DevilFish

DevilFish

D. ERIC HORNER

Order this book online at www.trafford.com
or email orders@trafford.com

Most Trafford titles are also available at major online book retailers.

Print information available on the last page.

ISBN: 978-1-4907-6267-8 (sc)
ISBN: 978-1-4907-6269-2 (hc)
ISBN: 978-1-4907-6268-5 (e)

Library of Congress Control Number: 2015911686

Trafford rev. 07/28/2015

 www.trafford.com
North America & international
toll-free: 1 888 232 4444 (USA & Canada)
fax: 812 355 4082

Dedication

THIS BOOK IS DEDICATED TO MY MOTHER AND FATHER, MARY DONNA AND DAVE. THANKS FOR ALWAYS BEING THERE FOR ME. WITHOUT YOUR INPUT AND UPBRINGING THERE IS NO WAY I WOULD BE THE RESILIENT MAN THAT I AM TODAY. I LOVE YOU BOTH VERY MUCH

Acknowledgement

TO MY NIECE, JUSTICE HATTAN, FOR
THE AMAZING COVER ART.

Introduction

T he Sun dropped and melted into the dark, turbulent Caribbean Sea, which made it very dark for Jonathan Silver and his first mate, Michael O'Connor, to negotiate the ship's deck. At least they blamed the darkness and cursed each wave that rocked the small boat named "Sammy" after Jonathan's daughter. Neither of them blamed the empty bottle of rum that rolled aimlessly on the deck, which the two head finished earlier. They had spent the day off the coast of Hispaniola searching and taking all of the treasures they could find from in the rich coral reef below their 35 foot floating fiberglass home. To say that these two fiftyish divers have had too much sun, rum, and fun on this three-day journey would be the understatement of the year.

"What made you want to come here," Michael asked slurring his words as the two round their way back and forth with the sea. Jonathan, the more experience sailor of the two, opened another small bottle of the coconut flavored rum to mix with and his Coca-Cola. If they were trying to look the part of "old salts" they were succeeding. They had been floating over the coral in this tropical paradise for four days. Jonathan took a much needed vacation from this job on Wall Street as a trader and had taken his best friend

Michael along. Michael, a Wall Street lawyer, was his trusted friend who handled the legalities of Jonathan's recent divorce.

"Why come all the way down here to hunt for shells? We could have done the same on Brighton Beach or the Jersey shore," Michael asked emphatically scrunching himself into his chair across the table from his friend. The two were a combination of sunburn and suntan, which contrasted greatly with their white hair and unshaved stubble on their faces. Jonathan's face and eyes told Michael everything he needed to know.

"Shells … is that all you'd think we are doing," Jonathan responded with an evil stare and the volume of someone who had been drinking.

"Well, that and sticking it to your ex, by going this far away."

The two men who were both in job positions where their appearance is crucial could care less in this island paradise. Today they were more than content wearing T-shirts and Bermuda shorts as opposed to their normal business attire, but anyone who knew them would be surprised.

Jonathan moves to the other side of the small table, so that he could see the eyes of his friend. "Do you really think that bitch has anything do with my plans?"

Michael worked on his drink, slowly, because he knew that he had enough. "I don't know what she had to do with it, but it is really strange for you to keep your down here when we have harbors and docks and water back home. This has to be a way to throw it in Judy's face, isn't it? I don't understand, Jonathan, I got you a hell of a settlement! You've got as much money from her parents estate as she did. And you got this boat. What's with you?"

Jonathan knocked back the remainder of his drink before sitting back down. The booze burned his throat as it went down and also fueled his machismo theory it's possible for friends to disagree and still stay friends, especially when the relationship has gone on for years. This is one of those relationships that quite honestly was why Jonathan and Judy didn't make it.

He reached across the table and forcibly grabbed at Michael's wrist. He squeezes it tightly while he asks a question. "Do you see the name of this boat? He was beginning to slur, it is not called Judy, but it's called Sammy, after my little girl. She's the world to me ...not that dried out old hag of a mother of hers!"

"So, you love your kid, who doesn't?"

"Yeah, but it's different for you Mike, your kids are teenagers and all grown up. That bitch kept her away from me during that time."

"That's why you got so much money. The court could see that she was screwing you over and using your daughter Samantha to do it. Forget about it, we are having a great time down here. I am anyhow; and I think I'm finally getting my sea legs."

Which was not true as the stumbled into his chair.

"You know what I want Jonathan? I want an adventure and this is adventure. Anchored out here with you getting drunk, it makes me feel like a pirate. I have enough money to be comfortable and so do you. I take back wondering why we're getting shells from here, this is way better than home."

Jonathan raised his eyebrows, makes another cocktail for each and settled in with a story. With the sun finally gone into the sea, it started to get dark in the small cutaway portion of the boat. Light began flickering in from the village on the island. It provided a dramatic backdrop for Jonathan's story.

"Adventure is what you're after," the captain questioned, slamming a crumpled piece of paper on the table. Here is an adventure!"

"What is this, a math to Blackboard's treasure," Michael laughed jokingly?

"In the 1500s this channel, well this whole area where we are anchored, was a popular shipping route. According to legend, a Portuguese boat and one of the French explorers crossed paths. A battle ensued and the Portuguese ship went to the bottom with all of its crew and treasure."

"I might be drunk, Jon, but I'm not 12. We've been diving around this area for three days and I haven't seen any old wrecked ship."

"It's down there. I came here on a cruise for my honeymoon 15 years ago. I talked to the locals and they verified the story."

"How much did you pay for the map? It's all bullshit man, if it wasn't, don't you think one of the locals would have scooped it up by now?"

"You see them and the way they live; they don't have the equipment or the time to look for it, for Christ's sake, they're worried about gathering food."

"Do you think that you are the only tourist that has been here? I mean the guy that sold you the map is probably laughing right now. I guess next you will be telling me some story about hammerhead sharks guarding the treasure. Now I have to take a leak, hold up on that story until I get back."

"Michael, do you have to go off the side? Then head is right over there."

"When I'm this drunk and wobbly, the side rail supports me. Don't worry it's not that long so the sharks will have no chance," he smiled and started urinating over the side. Jonathan could hear his friend taking care of this business and went back to concentrating on his rum. After what seemed like a long time, he heard a large splash, a faint scream for help, and then moved as quickly as he could to the side of the boat thinking his friend had toppled over.

When he got to the spot, Michael was gone. He searched the darkness frantically for his friend, shouting his name. "Michael, where are you buddy?" Jonathan's voice was scratchy from the alcohol, but he kept trying without hearing anything. He stumbled back inside and grabbed a flashlight to survey the shallow waters around the boat. He pointed the beam light directly where he thought Michael went into the water, but so no evidence of his friend. He cried out frantically this time. "Michael come can you hear me? Where are you man? This isn't funny!" Jonathan leaned as far as he could over the railing. He inspected the thick, white, fiberglass tubing that surrounded all of the walk ways around his boat. He didn't see any damage that might have caused Michael to go overboard.

"Where the hell could he have gone," he thought, shining the flashlight around all areas surrounding the boat.

Now his concern turned to anger as he felt that his drunken friend was just playing a trick on him. He decided that the reef that they were anchored to allowed him ample opportunity to get away and pull a prank if that was his intent.

"If that's how you are going to be; to hell with you," Jonathan swore to no one. "I'm going back inside."

He turned in and started to stomp away when he heard a ripple in the ocean water.

"Yeah, I figured as much," he thought to himself assuming that it was Michael. But it wasn't. They were anchored far enough from the coastline that there was no sound around, except for the faint ringing of a bell from a nearby buoy, marking the beginning of the reef.

Jonathan, a veteran skipper of these waters, started to get concerned because of the long quiet period of time he did not hear the constant crashing of waves. But in the years that he has known Michael this was by far the longest period of time for him to be silent. A strange mist or fog seemed to encompass The Sammy. It was like the vessel had been surrounded or engulfed by a cloud. The flashlight reflected back almost immediately and really wasn't helpful anymore, so Jonathan shut it off.

"Michael," he called with far less enthusiasm than before.

Jonathan heard something circle in the boat in the water. It wasn't a splash necessarily, just something surfacing and then going back under.

"Must be dolphin," he silently tried to convince himself, but deep in his heart he knew he was lying to himself. He turned his attention away from the noise and back to the eerie silence. All of a sudden, his head was filled with worry and concern for Michael. It's not like it had been before, but now it really seemed to hit him. *"I guess that he's not just fooling around. What happened to him?"*

Jonathan heard something come to the surface again. Although they had seen a number of dolphins when they were diving earlier, this didn't sound like it should. There was no splash like Jonathan had seen them perform before. Dolphins were terrific swimmers to be sure, but they were big creatures and no matter how smooth, they would make a noise. Whatever it was, it seemed to be circling.

He stared at the items on the table which they had gathered earlier. There were shells, big ones, and rocks as well as unusual pieces of coral. They were just souvenirs, kind of like something to collect because you have the time. Jonathan didn't feel that whatever was circling the boat had any reason to be upset, but he believed in ocean karma, and the old tales of the sea. He believed that what the sea creates should remain the sea. Maybe it was his hippie ideals and his love of the ocean coming out, but he really believed it. In fact he was planning on throwing the items they gathered back into the reef. Would he do that with the pirate's treasure he might find - hell no! Ideals are just that, the ideal way to do things and Jonathan felt he tries. He looked through the window again at the sea's treasures and turned his back to the railing when it happened.

As Jonathan stared at the items he heard a loud splash behind him. He tried to turn to look at the noise, but he couldn't turn his head. He didn't know what it was, but it had him! He felt the cold, slimy grip around his throat and gasped for air to cry out. Not even a squeak escaped his body and in a split second he was plucked off the starboard side of Sammy. Jonathan struggled, but it was pointless. Whatever had him was not going to be denied. He held his breath as long as he could and tried ripping from the grip; but it seemed every time that he squirmed free, there was another waiting arm of some kind. The last thing he remembered was feeling as if he had been trapped in an enclosed umbrella. Everything went black and he felt an excruciating pain in his skull.

Chapter 1

T he four young, fit looking, suntanned people were frolicking in the water off of Conger Island. Conger is one of the many almost man-made islands off the coast of Hispaniola. The island's purpose is mostly a port for passing cruise ships. Conger has built a large concrete structure as a dock for the passing gigantic ocean liners. The waters are crystal clear and located near a coral reef, which allows travelers to have a unique snorkeling experience. Travelers are also treated to some Latin flavor all along the dock. Before the dock construction was completed there were many skirmishes and flights between the locals as they argued over the best spots for their small shops. However, Samantha Silver and her three friends didn't care about the history of the dock or the struggles of the locals; they are here only for fun and frolic celebrating Samantha's 30th birthday. The place is perfect for what they want: shops, bars, restaurants and beautiful sunshine.

Samantha is tall compared to her friends, about 5'10". She played volleyball in high school, but since then was basically undecided on a career path. She has done lots of things to make ends meet, from waiting tables, to modeling, to office work, but she has never found what she would call a career. She has long dark hair, beautiful features, and light green eyes. She always thought that her eyes would set her apart from the other models, but New York City was filled with beautiful women and let's face it, by age 30, she realized that she would be at the end of a modeling career. Anyway Samantha is actually okay with that, and frankly enjoyed bouncing from job to job without a lot of responsibility. She went to college, but more because she felt she was supposed to than anything. She studied business, but only because the math requirements came easy to her. Her father Jonathan used to work with her when she was a little girl and she caught on quickly.

Then when she became a teenager, her father wasn't around very much. Samantha always assumed it was because of him, but they really became estranged because of her mother. She is down here now on the boat her father named after her, not to sign blame, but maybe find some answers to what happened to her dad. Her friends Jessica, a blond haired blue-eyed writer who works in the city and Macy, a young woman with closely cropped brown hair were along for the celebration. The three women were roommates at NYU and really best friends. The other member of this celebration, unfortunately, was Macy's constant companion, her boyfriend Chad. All four of the young adults are good looking and happy for the most part. I mean why shouldn't they be? Macy and Jessica have good jobs that they enjoy and Samantha, while her finances are pretty squared away thanks to her grandparents, lived all of her 30 years on the upper edge of middle-class and she is thankful, but not spoiled or satisfied.

In all actuality the tall, black haired beauty hasn't told her friends that the real reason they came here was because of a letter she had received from her father.

Macy circled and then surfaced climbing up on the back of the boat. "Man you guys, this is the most active snorkeling I have ever done. There is so much tropical sea life down there it's amazing," she announced to the other three already on deck. She grabbed a towel and chose the lounge chair in the middle.

"I know," Jessica agreed, "it's almost like an aquarium."

"I'm not sure; it doesn't seem that different than the Jersey shore."

"Chad, I don't believe you," Macy snapped, "it is the most beautiful coral reef I've ever seen in real life. The only reason you're along on this trip is because I didn't want to deal with you pouting and bitching over every little thing when I got back."

"If you throw him overboard, Sam and I promise not to tell."

"Hey, you would regret that Macy. I mean who would keep you company?"

"I don't know Chad," Samantha answered, "but there were quite a few staring at her in the bar last night."

Chad stood there looking down, smoking his cigarette because he knew Samantha was right. Their night last night at the bar had seen Macy strut her stuff in front of everyone, embarrassing the normally secure Chad.

"What's the matter Chaz," Jessica teased. "Yeah, it was fine when you were shaking your ass for those young the Latin girls."

"Thanks Sam, that was three whole days ago but thanks for bringing it up."

"No problem, I just wanted to help out."

"Why do I feel like you are all in this together?"

"Chad honey, what did you expect going on a week's vacation with all of us?"

Putting out his cigarette and putting on his sunglasses, and in his best New York accent replied, "I didn't expect you to be busting my balls all the time."

"Maybe they need busted. I mean, what guy goes on vacation with three girls just so he can watch his girlfriend?"

"That's not why I came down here Sam. I came down because I was worried for your safety ... all of you. You heard the stories about that a high school girl disappearing in the Caribbean; I wanted to make sure that didn't happen to you."

"Just the same," Macy butted in, "we are going out to dinner by ourselves tonight. Tomorrow is Samantha's birthday and we need a little girl time." Macy's comment caused the other friends off guard and they both were shocked that it even came up.

"Really, that's not fair. I mean what am I supposed to do?"

"You were a lifeguard on the Jersey shore dear, I'm sure you will think of something.

"Yeah, do you still have your little flags? You could signal to the shore from the boat."

"Good one Jessica. Those guys always thought they were such a big deal, doing this and that back and forth," Samantha added waving her arms to the delight of the other women.

Obviously Chad was upset and a little embarrassed. He reached for his cigarettes although he had just finished one. He lit up and replied, "Those little flags, as you guys call them, was our way of pointing out cute girls to the other lifeguards. Maybe I will just do the disco tonight."

It was obvious that he was doing whatever he could to make Macy jealous. It wasn't working however and she responded with, "Do you whatever you want to; I'm going to."

There was coldness in her voice and a look in her eyes that Samantha and Jessica had never detected before. Could she possibly be getting tired of Chad? The other girls hoped so, but didn't dare say anything. Instead the master conversationalist, and Jessica changed the subject.

"Hey Sam, can you really drive this boat?" With a smile, Samantha replies, "with the help of that GPS below and what my father taught me … you bet."

"I thought you weren't allowed to see your father," Macy asked.

"That didn't start until I was a teenager," Samantha answered.

"Was your mom afraid that your old man might do something to you?"

"Chad," his girlfriend exploded!!

"What? I heard he was a little different that's all."

"That would be a lot different, don't you think? And it would be sick too. Her dad wasn't a pervert, he just got burned out on Wall Street," Jessica pointed out, standing up for her friend.

Chad stood with the cigarette in his mouth and his palms face up as he shrugged the comment off.

"If that's true, then how old were you when you learned?"

Samantha put on her cover up and sunglasses as the sun continued to hang lower in the sky.

"Octopuses," she answered getting everyone's attention.

"What did you say," Jessica asked with a puzzled look.

"Octopuses … that was my father's true passion! Sure he loved being a successful Wall Street broker, but mostly he liked diving and snorkeling around this reef. We had money from my grandparents so even if he hadn't been successful we would have still vacationed down here."

"Did anyone see the amount of octopuses down there?"

The others just seemed to shake their heads and explained that that wasn't their purpose.

"I was watching Macy swooning around," Chad admitted.

"Oh please," Macy said rolling her eyes.

"No, I was and I was watching you other two as well. It's not every day that a man like me is able to see three women in their underpants doing scissor kicks."

"They are not underpants you fool they are swimsuits," Jessica pointed out.

"Same difference," Chad fired back, "especially when they are white."

Putting the conversation about the bathing suits aside, Macy focused the conversation back to the octopus.

"I'm glad we didn't see any of those. The octopus is freaky."

Instead of agreeing, Samantha kind of stood up for the creature.

"I used to feel the same way when I was a young girl down here with my dad. The now I'm not so sure. I mean I wouldn't want to have one on my face or anything, but they don't hurt people and I hear they are intelligent creatures. I see the way you are all looking at me, but my father used to catch them and put them inside of an aquarium so I could watch them move around. They are a little strange, but I would think to them we are strange too."

"Sam, you need a drink."

"I second that, Jessica," Chad piped with a smile. "Why don't we all disembark and go for a drink?"

"Hold on there mister. You are not going out with us ... remember?" Macy informed him.

Samantha ignored the couple's small squabble and got back on topic about the octopi that her dad used to bring her. "I used to sit and watch them all day while my parents were fighting it out. It actually relaxed me."

"I can't understand that," Jessica added. "Those things are like something from another planet. The way they can change colors and swim around is really gross."

"They call this island the breeding ground for the strangest animal on the planet. Chad was quick to join the conversation, as soon as Macy was finished explaining to him for at least the third time why he couldn't go out with the girls.

"You said that *they* saw - who is this *they* that everybody talks about?"

"It's the indigenous people of this island," Samantha answered. "I have been coming here since I was a little girl and there are all sorts of stories about this place."

"Stories," Macy asked, "about what?"

Samantha kind of dropped her head, looking at the deck of the boat, "Nothing, it's just stories. Let's and get cleaned up for dinner."

"I'm assuming this place on the pier specializes in seafood for dinner?"

"It depends on what they caught that day but I prefer the jerk chicken in this restaurant. It reminds me of my father."

"I'm sorry Samantha, this place must bring back a lot of memories."

"It's okay, they are not all bad. I think this was where my parents were happiest, but who knows," Samantha speculated.

Chad and Macy started making out and Chad started kissing her neck playfully. Macy didn't really resist; in fact she was playing along. The other girls could hear her teasing,

"Quit it."

Then they saw her hand move to the front of Chad's swimsuit. "How do you like it," Macy asked with a devilish smile on her face. "I promise we won't be late," she swore while kissing his face.

Chad knew that some more touching and kissing would get him what he wanted and for once it was not getting Macy into bed. He wanted to go to dinner with the girls. His begging and pleading was almost sickening. Macy put an end to it by making a suggestion. "I know that this was supposed to be our girls night out, but how about if he comes along but leaves us alone until dessert. That would give us our alone time and then Chad could be there for drinks."

Jessica and Samantha each looked at one another, rolled their eyes and then smiled and responded in unison, "We figured."

"I won't be in the way, I swear," Chad promised. "I'll watch from the bar then you just give me the signal when it's okay to come over."

"Is that okay with you guys," Macy asked. "If not just let me know and I will tell him he can wait until we get back. But Samantha, I wasn't sure if you would want to leave them roaming around on this boat."

"Yeah, I might try to drive it somewhere, you know for entertainment purposes."

Samantha knew that it was just a threat and not to take it seriously, but it did make her wonder.

The quartet took turns getting ready. With the lighting on the boat and the suntan they had all received earlier and a fresh shower, each of the women looked very attractive as they headed to kitchen area of the boat. They were busy chatting happily and wondering where Chad was. Macy yelled back to him and when they heard his response of still having to shave decided they had a little time to kill.

"Who is ready for a cocktail?" Macy played hostess and waitress, taking everyone's drink order and mixing the drinks. She also he yelled back to her boyfriend to find out why it was taking him so long. There was no answer, so she decided to take it a step further, barging in on him while he was shaving.

"Damn it Chad, what is taking you so long?"

"I couldn't get dressed right away. There is a young girl out there and I didn't know where the blinds are. So I've been going back and forth between the bathroom and bedroom to get dressed."

Macy looked out the window and sure enough there was about a young girl fishing right next to their dock. This upset Macy and she immediately exploded to her boyfriend.

"This is bullshit! I mean with all the places around here to fish, she has to be right here. I'm going to say something."

Macy went over to the sliding glass door and pounded on it loudly.

"Don't fish here, you dumb kid! Can't we have a little privacy?"

The young girl looked at Macy like she wasn't sure of what she was asking. Macy wondered if maybe she didn't speak English so she was gesturing while shouting.

"Get out of here! Scoot further down," she insisted. Macy figured that the young girl didn't know what she was trying to say, so she thought if she could give her a visual about where she needed to be that might help. She took a couple of strides towards the young lady when she saw something coming out of the water. She was pretty close to it, but still wasn't sure what it was. The strange object was about as big around as a man's leg and almost transparent in color. She noticed suction cups on one side and how incredibly nimble it was moving. What she saw caused her to cry out loudly and cover her eyes.

"Oh my God!"

Chapter 2

Jessica and I heard the scream by Macy and wondered what was happening. We took off to the back of the boat dodging the mess of towels and wet swimsuits along the way. It was not as challenging as I thought it would be because the interior of the boat is illuminated by the large street lights along the dock. We reached Macy at virtually the same time and could see the fear on her face and the panic in her eyes.

"Macy, what is it," I asked eagerly.

She didn't answer, just pointing to the main portion of the dock and stuttering aimlessly. She almost sounded like a little child.

"She must have seen something, but I can't get her to talk."

"You were back here for a while before," Jessica asked; "what is different on that dock?"

Chad shrugged his shoulders and kind of blew it off. "It just looks like a dock to me. The same place we have been tied up all week. I don't know what her problem is. Maybe she needs a drink."

I thought it, but didn't want to ask. I am the most outgoing of the three girls, but I am hands down the most polite and sensitive to others feelings, and Jessica is more brash. She is also closer to Macy and Chad then I am, so she can get away with speaking her mind.

9

"What the hell were you doing back here anyway? You were taking longer than a girl getting ready for prom." Chad wandered around and was very animated with his arms as he tried to explain. "I really don't know what her problem is. I was just back here getting ready and I guess I was taking too long. But I had to shave and everything and I couldn't just walk by the door to get my things," he explained.

As he was telling the story, Macy exploded like a shaken beer bottle.

"That's what it was. I remember now. There was a little girl, well not little, probably about 10 or 12 years old sitting on the pier and she could see in the boat and she was watching him. He did not want to parade around in front of this little girl in the buff, so he kept going back and forth between the bathroom and the bedroom."

"Then what happened to Macy," I asked.

She started explaining the most unbelievable story. It was something out of a horror movie. Macy claimed that a large arm, or something similar, rose out of the sea. It wrapped around the girl and quickly pulled her into the water. According to Macy, the area around the dock turned from clear blue ocean to blood red. It was hard to believe and Jessica dismissed it almost immediately.

"You mean like a sea monster or something?"

"I don't know what it was Jesse, I'm just telling you what I saw. There was no fight from the little girl until the thing had her in the water. Then I could see her struggling and splashing, but I guess it was too late, because the waters calmed down and then it was over. It happened so quickly, the girl didn't even stand a chance."

Jessica and I stood with our arms crossed in front of us looking skeptically at our old college roommate. "It's what happened guys, I swear. I know that you don't believe me, I can see it on your faces, but it happened."

"Just like when you and the counselor Mr. Reynolds were dating after summer camp?"

Macy knew that I had her and she came back with her patented defense. "Is that why you don't believe me because of one stupid teenage lie? This really happened and we should call somebody."

"Who should we call and what should we tell them? I mean there is no body, no evidence whatsoever to support your claim. Can you imagine us crying wolf now? What if we had a real emergency?"

"Maybe there is a body out there? I'm just not going to be the one to go out and look for it ... especially by myself."

With a lot of coaxing and promises from Chad, she reluctantly agreed to look as he headed to the restaurant. It didn't take us long to close in on the supposed abduction site. I was the first one to get there because I did not want this hanging over our evening or my birthday dinner.

"Is this the place right here," I questioned?

"Yeah, I think so. Do you see anything?"

Well I didn't, but I got down on my knees to look underneath a concrete structure. I noticed people disembarking from a huge cruise liner which had just recently docked. I guess for an overnight stay on the island. In my mind, I was disappointed to see a large ship and the crowds they bring.

"I guess my plans for a nice quiet birthday dinner with some friends are ruined. Even though these people had already paid for their meals, I knew that they would be flooding the pier and bars. They will also be hanging around tomorrow doing some excursions, which will be like children at recess. Not very relaxing."

"I don't see anything. Are you sure this is where it happened and Macy," I asked?

She nodded her head yes and I peeked over the side not wanting to get my black and white polka dot sundress wet or dirty.

"They'll be unloading that huge ship pretty soon, so we should get to the restaurant otherwise we will never find a seat."

Becoming a little bolder, Macy snuck a peek over the side and shook her head. Under her breath I could hear her say, "I really thought it was right here." Chad walked up to her and gave her a hug and a kiss on the cheek.

"Come on honey, we all see things from time to time. Maybe it was one of those visions you get in the desert, when you are hungry or thirsty."

Defiantly, even without any proof of her story, Macy fired back. "This was not a mirage, it was a real girl! It was horrible and gross, like nothing I had ever seen and no one believes me."

"I believe you honey. If you say it was there, then it was there."

"Don't patronize me Chad, just go along with the others if you want. I wouldn't blame you." The previous fight that Chad had some way weaseled out of seemed to start again.

"That figures," I thought, "it will never change with those two."

I put my feelings aside about Macy and Chad. For years the two of them have fought like cats and dogs and just when you think they are about to break up, Macy will tell you how wonderful Chad is. It is really frustrating and for the last year or so I have just been rolling with it, but it's beginning to bore me. Instead of focusing on those two, I decided to focus on my best friend Jess and my birthday.

The restaurant that we are eating at tonight is one of my very favorites. My dad would bring me here as a young girl and I remember it was like stepping into a different world. The décor is modern and clean with a ocean theme, but there is something different and special about this one. Maybe it's because of the location. It is way out on the end of the pier and depending on your table it almost feels like you are sitting on top of the water. There are windows on all sides of the restaurant and somehow they manage to keep them sparkling clean. Maybe that is what I like most about this place is the authenticity inside. My dad told me, many of the fishing equipment used to decorate the restaurant, has actually been used. I think many of the waiters speak Spanish or French or Portuguese and that sets the place apart. They all speak English, but it is broken and a struggle for many of them.

Besides all of that, it was always a special place for my dad and I to go. I can remember him sitting me on a bar stool next to him while we waited to be seated. I remember looking at the shiny, cherry wood finish on the long bar and the "characters" surrounding my father. I don't know if they were drawn to him, or if he to them, but there are always fishermen and boaters hanging out here. To me they looked and sounded more like pirates. Every one of them that I can remember, seemed to have a distinctive laugh and they all smoked and smelled of liquor. Some might think that this sounds awfully frightening to a child, but I looked at it differently. My dad would stand me on a bar stool to speak to everyone, like he was showing me off. It was that time when I felt the most pride and love in my father's eyes and that surely makes a little girl feel good.

"What are you thinking about Samantha?"

"Nothing just remembering fondly back to my childhood. This used to be our place - my Dad and I. When he knew it was time to take out the boat we would always make a point of coming here. It was and still is so much fun ... you never know what is going to be on the menu or who might be stopping by. I still hear that this was a surly place, but I never had any trouble in here. Maybe that's because my father was always with me."

"Maybe no one hassled you because your Dad was with you. God, I just realized that I don't know much about your father. I mean we were roommates and everything and I feel terrible not ever asking about your personal life.

"Forget it Jesse, let's get a table."

Chapter 3

We navigated the crowded room, not so crowded with people as it was with relics from another time. There were large compasses and maps and telescopes everywhere. It was a complete maze to get to a hostess stand but surprisingly, we were seated quickly and I thought to myself that the large cruise ship had probably not started unloading yet. The four of us sat there looking over the menu while also viewing the rising and falling ocean. To me it was hypnotic …. always had been ever since I was a little girl. It's as soothing as the ticking of a clock or a metronome.

If I could hear the waves crashing, I'd be fast asleep."

Macy noticed that I was in a little bit of a trance and secretly ordered a round of rum shots. She has always been the one to keep the party rolling in our group. I like to drink, not as much as the other girls, but I never understood the ceremony of taking a shot of liquor with everyone else. It always seemed a little immature to me especially at our age. Sure, we are only in our early 30s, but this seemed more like something we would do in college. Although I didn't like the tradition, I went along with this like everyone else.

"This is for Samantha. I hope that you have a wonderful birthday and hope that it is a memorable one."

Shouts of here - here and birthday wishes from strangers including the waitress, Frederica, got the evening started. Our meal started with appetizer orders of the fried calamari and we continued to search the extensive menu of delicious seafood entrees. The calamari was a hit until Jessica asked what it was and I explained it.

"It is deep-fried squid," I explained. "Come on, you guys knew that." I did read the disgust on some of their faces and Chad even spit his mouthful back into his napkin.

"What's wrong? I mean you guys act like you never had it before."

"Oh, we've had it before but after what I witnessed today, it doesn't seem that appealing," Macy added with a wrinkled nose while ordering another round of drinks.

"I don't think any of us know what you really saw Macy," Jessica pointed out.

"I don't really know what it was, but it could have been the arm of a squid."

We all started laughing and Jessica pointed out, "They are not usually called arms, but rather tentacles."

Trying to laugh it off, Macy replied, "Testicles I always thought those were some place else.

Chad, never one to miss out on a sexual innuendo fired back, "They are and I like the way you are thinking. Bartender, another round for our table please."

The entire meal was filled with that kind of happiness and lively conversation. Maybe the booze got things rolling, but once we started, we were back in our college days. The meal was tremendous from the appetizer, to the deep fried grouper which I had, to the crab legs and lobster tail that the others devoured. It was certainly a messy meal and our dining area showed it. We had shells and scraps from what looked like every animal in the sea. This is just how I wanted to celebrate my birthday with great friends and wonderful memories of this special place.

I sat quietly thinking back to when I was a little girl. I used to watch the adults around us having such a great time, laughing and talking and I wondered why my parents sat in silence or argued over nothing so loudly that I wanted to crawl under the table and hide. I relished in the fact that I might be one of those patrons now that I was so envious of years ago. A small smile came across my face and even though Macy was starting to get ripped, the everyone could tell something was wrong.

"Is there something wrong," she asked?

"Quite the opposite," I answered, "you see when ..."

That was all she needed to hear and cut me off in the middle of my sentence.

"Cool, I thought maybe you weren't having a good time and it is your birthday. Come on let's get another shot. This Sailor Jerry stuff is great!"

I have known Macy since before our college days and from past experience, she will get this certain look on her face and the rest of us know we are in for a long night. She had that look right now!

Trying to force some more butter and bread on her, I offered her some more rolls. Unfortunately she said that she was full. Chad begged me to leave her alone, so I did and hours later we were still at the restaurant. The crowd from the cruise ship had come and gone and the only people remaining were the old guys at the bar. Jessica, Chad, and I all had our fill of rum and I was trying my best to get them to leave. That's when a guy, an old guy who looked like he made his living outdoors, sauntered up. His face was weathered from his time spent in the wind and the sun. That combined with his hard drinking had formed deep grooves in his face. As he came closer and got into the light, he looked more like he was wearing a mask that you would see on Halloween. His ears and nose were too big for his small head and short body. He didn't walk with a limp, but had the peculiar habit of stopping every three or four steps to regain his balance. I had this strange feeling that I knew him for whatever reason. But I didn't spend a whole lot of time this evening looking around, so I don't know how far he came. Like a trekking torpedo, he continued his journey over to our seats. There are not many tables with customers remaining, so it was not a surprise that he introduced himself and asked to sit with us.

"My name is Rollings, may I join you?" To say that his voice is gruff would be an understatement. I started to back away from the table, but soon felt his rough hand clasp around my wrist.

"Um... we are getting ready to leave. My friend has had too much to drink." Even though what I said was true, I was more or less just trying to avoid this guy.

"Don't rush off Samantha," the old guy smiled gripping my wrist tighter.

"Let go of me," I snapped pulling away my arm. How do you know my name anyhow?"

The man pulled out his rolling papers and a small tin of tobacco. Without answering he started to roll a cigarette. It looked like hell, all crumpled and uneven with tobacco hanging carelessly out the tip. It's a far cry from the ones that Chad smokes. He lit one end and took a long drag. With smoke coming out of his nose and mouth he finally answered.

"I am a good friend of your father's. I played a big part in setting *The Sammy* up. I spent hours with your father teaching him how to drive that boat and navigate the waters in this area." He accentuated his point with a phlegm-filled hack before taking another hit, finishing his entire makeshift cigarette. I was more than a little skeptical. I mean I don't remember this guy at all and if he would have spent all that time around my Dad, I think I would have.

"Did you find it yet?"

The guy was starting to get on my nerves and give me a creepy feeling.

"Find what, you old pervert," I shouted loudly as to draw attention, which it did at least from Chad. "Are you bothering the lady old man?" Chad yelled.

With an inquisitive look through his deep set grayish eyes, which almost matched what little hair he had on the top of his head and his handle bar mustache, Rollings shrugged his shoulders and answered, "I'm a friend of her father's. I don't think I'm bothering her, but who the hell are you anyway?"

Chad took the old man's statement as some sort of personal challenge. He fired that with the combination of alcohol and New

York City bravado, "Who am I? Let's go outside and I'll show you who I am, you salty old prick!"

"You guys… let's tone it down a notch," I suggested, noticing people around us looking.

I don't think that Chad remembered that we were in an another country and who knows if this old guy could have a gun. He is probably friends with everybody in here and we were the strangers. Thank goodness Macy came to my rescue with nonsense conversation.

I really was not interested in what they planned to do or their sex life in general, so I offered Mr. Rollings a chair. He smiled brightly and unfortunately for the old guy, his teeth looked as bad as the cigarettes that he was rolling.

"Thank you, but it's not Mr. anything, it's just Rollings. You see I picked up that name because I roll my own cigarettes, have been doing that since I was 16." By the look on Jessica's face, we were both thinking the same thing, but she was one that said it.

"How long ago was that?"

"Ha ha, longer than either one of you two have been alive that's for sure. Sam, you are probably about 30 now. I wish you guys could have seen her back then. What a pistol, just like her dad. I can still see them in the bar, her on a stool reciting poetry. Everyone would cheer which made her dad so proud. I never thought he would be foolish enough to do what he did."

Chad and Macy moved in a little closer to hear the old man's forced speech. He knew how to get people into the story. He talked softer and softer until everyone was where he wanted them to be. I had just enough liquor to be bolder than normal.

"If you're talking about divorcing my mom, that's right it was stupid."

"No, that wasn't very smart, but that's not what I mean at all."

He had all of our attention now and he knew it. He was just waiting for someone to ask the question. Playing it up dramatically, he ordered another drink for himself and a round for all of us. Macy, the drunkest and most outspoken of the group took the bait and ran with it.

"Well then what was the dumbest thing?"

The old man's eyes brightened as he knocked back the shot. It seemed like he had been waiting 20 years to tell the story. I have to believe that he intentionally talked a little softer, to make us all move in and pay attention.

"Your father loved this island of Conger. He loved it even more after I showed him how to navigate these waters. I guess the stress from his job and that city was just wearing on him. I don't understand that but I have never been to a city. Nope, I have spent all my life right here. Well, so far anyway."

I got the feeling that the old man was drifting and loved being the center of attention, so I felt it might be good for me to keep him on track. "Rollings, what about my father?"

"Your father," he questioned and paused? "Oh that's right, his biggest mistake was not getting divorced from your mother ... it was going after the treasure." He accentuated his announcement by slamming another shot. It was obvious to me that this old sea dog was just making shit up now to keep us interested.

"Come on guys," I suggested. "Let's give the old guy his space, he looks like he could use the oxygen. Good to meet you - maybe we will be back sometime. Thanks for that drink and teaching my dad all about this part of the world. I think it extended his life by about 10 years."

The women started gathering their purses and preparing to leave, when the old man perked up again. "Samantha, how did your father die?"

Everyone in the group stopped getting ready to leave and looked directly at me. I didn't choke on it, but thinking about Dad's death, even for a second was troubling. "He died of a heart attack."

"Are you sure about that," he baited me. "Is that what the doctor said, Samantha?"

Now I was starting to get a little pissed off. And who knows if this old drunk guy is telling me the truth? But the truth is that I was estranged from my dad during my teenage years.

"It was a combination of my mother and me being too wrapped up in my own life to demand that I saw him. The truth is I took my

mother's word at face value and never looked any further. Before now, I head no reason to doubt her, but maybe I should look into it."

The man took out a gold coin, showed it to everyone and then placed it in front of me. Everyone, except for me, was impressed and gasped. I could tell by the looks on their faces that now they wanted more.

"Is that real," Macy inquired?

"It feels real to me," Chad stated, letting it bounce off of the table onto the floor.

"I have never seen a coin like this," Jessica said her blue eyes opening widely." Where did you get it?"

Ordering another round, Rollings quickly became the center of attention. For my money that's all the old guy wanted. I could be wrong but that was something my father warned me about years ago. If he said it once, he said that a thousand times.

"Sammy, there are all sorts of wild stories around this island. Mostly they spring from folklore and fear by the locals … don't believe all of it."

"My dad told me all about the stories and all that local bullshit. I don't believe a word of it. You could have bought that coin at one of the bazaars somewhere on the island.

"Come on guys, we don't have to listen to this."

Rollings took his time pulling out his tobacco and paper. He rolled up another one, took a big drag and for effect blew the smoke directly into the air. He clapped his dry, chapped hands together before rubbing his face.

"Remember when I first approached you, I asked if you had found it yet. What did you think I was talking about? You have seen another coin like this on the boat, haven't you? Perhaps you ran across a coin like this on top of a map in the galley. Maybe you found a coin like this in Jonathan's bed. Either way it doesn't really matter, you know about it now.

I was fuming. I had found many coins like this placed strategically around the interior of the boat. I didn't know what they meant and I still don't. My father was down here with one of his friends the last time ... right before his heart attack. At least that's what mom said. This guy is just playing with me, I know it.

With authority and volume I promised, "You tell me what you know, you old bastard, or I will scratch your eyes out!" My loud threats surprised even my own friends, let alone the people at the bar. Rollings sort of smiled and clasped his hands together and held his index fingers on the bridge of his nose, smiling wickedly.

"You seem a little tense to hear the truth. Besides, you probably wouldn't believe it anyhow."

"I'll believe it, tell me," Chad asked, sitting on the edge of the chair like a dog begging for a treat.

"I'll believe it also ... come on," Macy said. Jessica seemed to be the only one on my side.

"I don't know you guys. I mean what if it makes her dad looked like a clown?"

"Thanks Jesse," I answered.

Like a spooky fortune teller Rollings enticed everyone even further. "I have all the proof right here in my pocket."

Chapter 4

T he proof which Rollings had was in the form of a tattered map and a story that was good only on this Caribbean island. I really am not sure if I believe him or not, but he sure as hell did.

"Your father, Jonathan, has a map just like this one on your boat. It is my belief that he was killed by the keeper of the treasure."

Jesse and I rolled our eyes and I shot back at him. "You are either drunk or crazy, my father died of a heart attack."

He was offended by not only my accusation, but because I interrupted his story. He squinted his eyes which made the wrinkles more visible, making his face looked like a roadmap. He looked at me in disbelief since I was not buying his story.

"But the coins ... where would I have gotten them if not from the treasure? I have taken them to the bank and verified that they are from the 1500s."

"I could walk down the pier and find the exact same thing in one of the shops," I promised. I stood up and told my friends, "Let's get out of here. I don't think that we need to listen to anymore of this bullshit."

My friends and I started leaving the restaurant and Rollings blocked my path.

"Samantha, wait, I have something else in my pocket."

"That sounds like a proposition, and I don't want to see that little thing," I assured him.

He sort of smiled reaching into his other pocket and pulled out a notarized death certificate, signed by the Conger Island medical examiner. "Does this convince you at all?"

I looked it over and it seemed authentic, but then again so did the coins. "You could have gotten this at a jewelry or souvenir store along with those coins."

"Would I have told the coroner's office to make this up also, my dear," he confidently asked.

I moved in closer to see what he was pointing at and it was proof … at least for me. The death certificate revealed an old family secret that I'm sure he didn't share with his fishing buddy. Many years ago, in 1983 when the stock market tanked a client of my fathers took the slump out on him physically. He surgically removed all his toes, one by one. Dad was so painfully embarrassed by this and for years he felt like he deserved it, since he had given this guy bad advice and it cost him his life savings. The guy made threats to the rest of the family, so no one ever went to the police. He told the hospital then it was some sort of home repair accident in, but all of us knew better. I don't really believe that he ever recovered from the shame of being too scared to say anything. It haunted him until the end.

"Are you convinced now," he asked.

I was starting to get tired with this guy but I wanted him to just tell me what was on his mind.

"You didn't know about that, you couldn't have. It means nothing."

My friends started gathering around to see what was on the paper and I was trying to respect my father's privacy, so I grabbed the death certificate quickly from the old sailor's hands.

"While you have that in your hands, why don't you show me where it says cause of death was a heart attack."

I scanned a little higher on the page to the cause of death and I was shocked!

"What happened and if this is right, who could have done this," I wondered silently?

I read the cause of death and his skull had been punctured repeatedly almost like someone hit him with an ax. There was no mention of a heart attack anywhere. In fact they listed the cause as "unknown".

"Do I have your attention now," Rollings smugly asked? "May I finish my story?"

I really didn't have any choice but to let him continue. I did my best sending off my friends that were looking over my shoulder. I nodded my head towards him and he continued.

"You see there is a treasure, a virtual fortune in these gold coins located beneath this pier. It's not that the locals don't know it's there, they are just too scared to go get it."

"Just what are they afraid of," I asked?

Lighting another one of his homemade specials, Rollings answered. "Devilfish! It's not the hammerhead sharks, or blues that keep them away from the treasure. Many men have been eaten by them so it is definitely the fear of the devilfish. That's what I believe got your father. It wasn't a heart attack, although maybe he would have been better off."

"How do you know," I asked.

He stroked his beard and scratched his neck as if the itching was driving him crazy.

"I know because we have seen it. Did you know that octopi can lie on the ocean floor? It's because they have no bones. Yeah, one the size of a deer can squeeze through a door opening not any bigger than that." He held up his index finger and thumb about an inch apart to accentuate his point. He had every single one of us waiting on his every word.

"How big," Chad asked?

"Six feet maybe more … it's hard to tell with those damned things. You see they have very special skin. Their skin has pores that open and close whenever the beast wants to perfectly camouflaging its movements. I saw that thing when I was done being with your father and I'm not ashamed to tell you that I was scared.

Chad and Macy were hypnotized, Jessica still had a bit of skepticism as did I.

"What makes you so sure that this thing killed my father?"

"Do you see there right below the cause of death? It says that trace amounts of a dark, unknown liquid was also found. I contend that this liquid is the octopus' defense discharge. And there have been more than a few unknown deaths or murders around here lately."

"That doesn't mean anything. They are probably not even related," Jesse proudly pointed out.

The fishermen knew that he had his work cut out for him, to convince us. He ordered another drink and threw it back and then he leaned in to all of us. I could smell the liquor on his breath from 3 feet away.

"Many of the fishermen do the old style net fishing … throw it out there and take whatever you haul in." The whole group was shaking their heads in agreement showing that understood.

"Since your father died, Samantha, there have been at least a dozen bodies pulled out of these waters right here … all unexplained deaths. Not all of them were even going after the treasure. There are reports that I have heard about something reaching out of the water and snatching people that were even remotely near the treasures. I just thought you should know how your father died, especially considering where your boat is parked.

"Nice meeting you again Samantha."

He ended our meeting much more politely than it started and Rollings limped slowly away. I didn't remember noticing the way he walked earlier, because before our conversation, I paid no attention to this old guy. He certainly gave me a lot to think about with his stories of the sea in regards to my father's death.

"Was he here hunting treasure? Is that what my mother hated most? Why did he choose to house the boat down here anyway? I have found no evidence of a mistress. Maybe he was searching for this treasure and just maybe this thing, whatever it is, killed him."

"Are you okay, Sam," Jesse asked with genuine concern.

I shook my head yes, but really I wasn't. I felt cold inside. I'm not sure why. Maybe it was his callousness about dad. That guy didn't even seem surprised or shocked looking at the death certificate. Or maybe I felt cold inside because my father was spending more time with this clown than working on building his family. Either way, it didn't matter. I crossed my arms in front of me in a defensive posture after running my fingers through my long, black hair and I was thrilled when Chad was the first to mention that if was time to be heading out. Normally he is the night owl of the group, but I suspect he had other things on his mind.

I'm sure it was obvious to Macy as well. The two of them argued playfully about picking up the bill, but in the end it was neither. The trust fund baby as we like to tease Jesse had already instructed the wait staff that she would be paying.

"Thanks Jesse, I hope that you had fun. I know that I did."

"Of course I did but what's up with that old guy," she asked as we watched Macy and Chad play grab ass from light pole to light pole down the pier.

I took a deep breath to relax a little and then it all came pouring out. "I've always been angry with Jonathan. I blame him for the divorce with my mom and for having this boat this far away ... for shutting me out of his life. I didn't think that he gave a damn about me."

Over all the noise of juvenile flirting that was happening around us, Jessica asked, "Does the way that he died makes that much difference?"

"You have probably never been turned away from anything. I mean look at you, with your blonde hair, blue eyes and great figure and besides all that - you are rich."

We strolled along aimlessly kidding with each other and yelling at Chad and Macy to get a room, as they made out passionately every four or five steps. Their behavior was the only reason that I noticed a fisherman floating in his rickety looking, small wooden boat.

He had a long fishing pole and was sitting there like a statue in a garden. We were not even aware that below the surface was a whirlpool being created following along the same path as Chad and Macy. The underwater activity would stop when they did and then start up again when the lovebirds moved along. I looked up from the water and waved hello to the fishermen. That's when I noticed the strange activity in the water. It was almost like something down there could see. I put that thought out of my mind.

"Samantha, it's dark out, you've been drinking, there is no way that something could see out of the water," I told myself.

But the more I watched the water, the movements seemed to move at and exact match to Macy and Chad's movements on the dock. The cold feeling that had left me once I stepped down in the warm Caribbean night returned in a flash. Chad had started showing off for his girlfriend acting like a teenager. I could hear them starting to disagree. For any other couple the disagreement would be considered an argument, but for these two kids the way they communicate is by yelling at each other.

"Chad, quit trying to show off, you're drunk!" Macy stopped near one of the overhead lamps… which is why I probably noticed that whatever was trailing the two stopped momentarily, and then began moving again when she did.

Chad uttered that famous phrase while offering to do tricks. "I am not drunk. Macy, watch me walk a straight line." Rather than choose a solid joint in the concrete pier to show off his prowess, Chad chose the side of the pier. He was doing a good job of balancing, but it obviously took a lot of effort.

"Get down from there," yelled Macy.

"You want me to jump in? If that's what you want I will."

"Don't you dare," Macy warned, "that is the only good outfit that you brought! Just get down, Chad." Chad took the opportunity to get away from the edge and start dancing to his own music.

"I'm getting down Macy, what do you think? Does it make you want me? How about this move, does it make you want me?" As hard as it was to not focus on Chad and Macy and their weird foreplay, I was focused on the water. The swirling head stopped again and I squinted hard to try and see something under the water. Jessica took time out from talking about herself to ask me what I was looking at.

"Is there something in the water, Sam?"

"I'm not sure but something seems to be following them and us too for that matter."

"I don't see anything," Jessica promised. "Come on, we are almost back to the boat, you and I can sit and talk while those two get it over with."

"That's a good idea; I'll make us some coffee."

I heard Chad blurt out a challenge to his girl. "First one undressed and in bed gets the first happy ending!"

"There is no need to race, jackass ... you'll always finish before me!"

"You guys," I yelled, moving along the pier "it's my birthday celebration. I thought we might play a game or something!"

I wasn't paying any attention to the water anymore, but the fisherman was. Not for the same reasons as I was and then he yelled up to us. "For Christ's sake children; how is anyone supposed to catch anything with all that yelling? This is my livelihood ... it's how I make my money and you guys come down here, get drunk and think that the world is your oyster. Let me tell you..."

Jessica and I strolled away waving to the fishermen. "Sorry sir," I yelled to him, but Jesse took it a step further by mooning him ever so briefly. "I hope this makes up for it," she teased quickly putting her sundress back down.

The guy laughed and then started asking for more. We giggled like little spoiled brats and decided to run to the boat. We each slipped off our sandals and ran as quickly as we could. When I was removing my sandals, for some reason I looked into the water. The water was swirling and rapidly moving towards the boat. I couldn't really hear much over our giggling as we were running away, but I thought that I heard a noise from the water and just brushed it off.

A long ocean colored arm rose from the dark water into the small marina area. The fishermen never saw it ... he was too busy wiping water out of his eyes that seemed to come from below. With one swoop of that arm the fishermen was quickly knocked out of the boat. His glasses were thrown off and he was certainly surprised to find himself in the water. He thrashed and splashed, holding his breath and trying to get his bearings. He saw his small wooden boat drifting away from him as the tide swept it away. Without his glasses, combined with the darkness, he had no idea where he was. He felt something brush against his leg and thought maybe it was his anchor string. He reached for it and what ever it was slipped threw up his hands. He threaded water, keeping himself from going under and frantically tried yelling for assistance.

"Somebody help me please! I lost my glasses and my boat! Help me please!"

Unfortunately for the fishermen no one was close enough to come to his aid. He started getting tired, holding himself above the surface. He felt another nudge, this time on his other leg and baths when the panic really set in. He thought that maybe a shark was circling in the marina. He had seen them circling because of the scraps of bait thrown into the water by other fishermen.

Just the thought of a shark circling terrified him. His heart rate quickened and suddenly the tepid Caribbean waters felt ice cold. He felt something go by him again and this time he looked into the water trying to make out the image. He was able to see the shape of the creature circling him and it wasn't a shark. He breathed a quick sigh of relief, but only for a split second. Then he felt something grab his feet. He wasn't able to tread water anymore and got as much air as he could before he was dragged under. He flailed his arms wildly trying to fight back, but whatever it was that had him wasn't letting go. It dragged him completely under and was obviously pulling him wherever it wanted. Of course he couldn't see in the murky salt water especially without his glasses at night, but the last thing he remembered was being eye to eye with a large body mass of something.

"But it had eyes," he was thinking before he was engulfed on all sides by something.

He tried reaching for the surface but it was in vain. Not only was he out of oxygen and about to drown, but whatever this <u>thing</u> was, it seemed to be fracturing his skull. In a matter of moments the life and death struggle was over and the winner dragged the limp, water logged body of this fisherman to add to the collection near his lair and the sunken treasure.

Chapter 5

The huffing and puffing that had been going on, on the lower deck, of my boat for a full 15 minutes was finally over. Jessica and I sat above conversing and sipping our coffee.

"That was a long session for those two," Jessica smiled.

"You have to remember that Chad was drinking."

"Do you remember how quick with a used to be when we lived together? I'll tell you, Sam, that seems like forever ago."

"It kind of was," I answered. "I mean it was over five years ago, which might not seem like a long time, until you realize that we are only 30."

"Yes, you're right, but you never think of what you want to do it until it's too late. Take me for example ... I thought that I would be all over the tabloids by now. Either I would be married to a handsome prince, or a model or someone very intercontinental and worldly."

"That's what I love about you Jesse, such low standards."

"Okay then what about you, you had to have something you wanted to do?"

"The way you are talking, it's like we are too old. I'm not too old. I'm in the best shape that I ever have been in and I feel great."

Jessica gathered their empty mugs and floated around the galley like she knew what she was doing. I knew better than that, this girl hasn't spent any time at all in the kitchen, but seem to be enjoying herself.

"Okay Ms. Fitness what do you want to do?"

I thought about it, but to be honest this is the only time that I had. I didn't have a good answer or even a poor one. I was embarrassed for not having an answer. But I thought back to tonight and meeting Rollings and I knew what I really wanted. A shy smile came across my lips. For the first time in my 30 years I knew what I wanted to do. I went into the galley and grabbed the map that my father had purchased all those years ago. I took that and the coin to where Jessica was standing.

"I want to follow in Jonathan's footsteps. I want to find this treasure."

"You can't be serious Sam. If that old guy was even close to being right, you don't want that to happen you. I mean that's the dumbest idea I've ever heard," Jesse quipped in an angry tone.

I was contemplating her feelings, but the truth was that I really didn't know what happened to my dad. That certificate might be a fake and there certainly are shots like that all over the island. I guess what I was thinking or trying to convince myself of was that there really isn't danger looking for that treasure.

"What was I doing? It would have made sense doing this right after dad died, but why now? I guess a couple of reasons." I argued with myself, *"if Jonathan died looking for this treasure, it must exist. My father was a lot of things, but never a liar. Secondly, this may be my last chance for an adventure. I just turned 30 and really have never done anything along these lines before. My friends are already down here with me so this would be the perfect time,"* I thought trying to convince myself.

"That's about the response I would expect from a little rich girl. I mean haven't you ever wanted to do anything wild?"

Her blue eyes pierced me like daggers and then showing her polite private school upbringing, she fired back, "Only all the time! Being a little rich girl isn't all you make it out to be."

"I know I have seen you struggle with using the right fork at the club," I joked. I looked down, laughing at my own joke, but obviously Jess didn't see the humor.

"You know that I have always wanted to get out from under the stranglehold my parents have on me. It would do me good to find some sort of treasure and use it any way I want to."

I could begin feeling her coming over to my side. "Then what is the problem," I asked?

I have known her long enough to be able to tell when she is holding something back. She had a look of both innocence and shame on her face while she admitted, "I'm scared. Is that okay? I've never done anything like this."

"Neither have I," I promised, "isn't that kind of the point? Neither of us really needs the money and neither did my old man, but where is your pioneer spirit and curiosity?"

"It seems to be leaving me the more sober that I get."

"We can dive during the day time and you can just snorkel on the surface if you don't want to scuba. We just need to spot the treasure and then we can come back to get it later." I could tell that something else was bothering my friend, I didn't even need to ask, I just shot her a look.

"There is something else, Sam. What about those things? I mean are they dangerous?"

"Hammerhead sharks," I asked? "Yeah, they can be deadly. If you stay close to me, I have one of those bang stick things that work really well." It isn't really the sharks. I know they are dangerous, but they should leave us alone."

"Then what is the big problem?"

"I'm worried about that devilfish thing! They are a really strange and dangerous creature and now that I realize one is guarding the treasure; I don't want to have anything to do with it. Those things are smart ... researchers feel that they may be smarter than dolphins."

I smiled easily at her. "Have you ever really seen one? I mean they really aren't that big. And speaking of not all that big," I joked as Chad entered the room.

"Get bent Samantha, I just checked on your former roommate and now she is sleeping satisfied. What are you guys talking about anyway?"

"Samantha wants to look for that sunken treasure that old guy was talking about at the restaurant."

"Cool … do you guys want to start looking tonight? Unlike my lady, I'm ready to go."

"Hey genius, did you forget what Macy told us she saw right out of that patio door?"

I wasn't sure if Chad was just trying to be macho, or is he truly had forgotten. He's not the sharpest tool in the shed, so he may have forgotten. It started coming back to him; I could see it on his face. "Oh, you mean that little girl? I wouldn't put a whole lot of faith in what she was saying. You guys have lived around her longer than me, so you know sometimes she exaggerates."

What Chad said actually made some sense but when I started thinking back to the story she had told which matched with Rollings', I started thinking that it was possible. I certainly was not going to share than with Jessica, but I was intrigued.

"How big would the arms have to be?" I thought silently. "I wound guess at the least 6 feet for them to be out on the pier and swiping something off of it …like a person. I have heard lore that giant octopi may live out in the middle of the ocean, but never this close to the land. I couldn't really share any of what I'm thinking with Jessica; she would just freak. Maybe for once Macy was telling the truth."

Chad had already made his decision and darn good move towards the back of the boat.

"Where are you going," Jesse asked?

Chad sort of puffed out his chest and grabbed his snorkeling gear. "I'm going to get rich. Make my money the pirate way and find that treasure."

Even though Macy was still sound asleep and I could really give a damn if he was eaten by sharks or a devil fish, or even drown … I couldn't let that happen to my friend's guy.

"You're not going anywhere at this hour," I instructed. "It's too dark anyhow and I'm still the captain."

"I don't get it," Chad complained with his mask on the top of his head. "We had that map and everything so what's the big deal?"

"The big deal is we can't see anything down there. It would just be a pointless exercise!

Even while we were dating, I thought you were smarter than that."

"How about that," I thought to myself, I never knew that you two were an item."

"Wait … you guys went out," I asked?

Jessica rolled her eyes and fessed up. With a deep exhale she admitted that it was only a couple of times. I was still stunned! I mean Jesse and I are certainly better friends than her and Macy, but we were all roommates together. I gave her a parental look and she started blurting out the details.

"It was a long time ago in college, and the two of them were having problems and I don't know, I was trying to make her jealous to want him back. It was a stupid plan and I have regretted it ever since."

"It was a great plan," Chad added gleefully. "It worked …didn't it?"

I was completely blown away. I didn't know anything about this, probably because I was too wrapped up in my own life at that time. "Did you guys, you know," I asked?

"Like rabbits; the girl is insatiable."

"Did you ever think Chad, that you were not satisfying me … that's why?"

I could believe what I was hearing and now I'm trapped on a small boat with these guys. I needed a moment to take in everything. If I would have known, I never in my life would have allowed him to come with us. I guess if they're cool with that I should be also, but it puts me in a more commander position. I'm not going to let those two be alone at all.

"Macy is okay with all of this," I asked?

"Once she found out I did it to get her back, she understood."

"You don't have to make it sound like such a conquest, Chad. There was never anything to it."

"That's true both ways, Jesse. Now... are we going to look for this sunken treasure or not?"

The two of them are actually acting more like Macy and Chad than anything. It was strange. The other thing is Jessica is rich and pretty and Chad would drop Macy in a heartbeat to be with her. I have to make sure that I don't leave them alone... not that they would be together, but so they don't drown each other."

In response to Chad's request to begin our sunken treasure hunt I responded, "I don't think that after what we had to drink tonight it would be a good idea. So just hold on and we will start first thing tomorrow." It was not hard to see the disappointment on Chad's face and hear it in his voice as he walked towards the back of the boat.

"This is bullshit! You are not in charge of what I do. If I want to go looking at night, I should be able to."

I followed him out onto the sunning area and flicked on the lights. We continued arguing about me being in charge and it being my boat and suddenly I saw something moving in the water. It was that exact same whirlpool that I had seen earlier, circling the fisherman's boat. I looked out into the harbor to see if he was still around, but he wasn't. A light fog had started to drift in and the horn from a passing oil tanker added to the eerie feeling that surrounded me.

"What happened to that fisherman," I wondered silently still arguing with Chad. "This would be the perfect time to be out here, especially if he wanted peace and quiet... at least according to my father."

He always loved fishing at this time of day, or should I say time of night. I'm really not sure why, but all the locals did. To me, I always felt it was a little scary. At first I thought it was just because I was a kid, but it's even spookier now, especially with this fog and that eerie horn blowing.

"Maybe that's what happened to the fisherman," I wondered. "Maybe he drifted into the path of one of those ships. But that really didn't make sense, he was just stationed there fishing away. Had he just moved on to an another fishing spot? Maybe he fell out of his boat and

*the sharks got him. I looked frantically with the searchlight into the
water looking for his boat."*

"You're not going to find that treasure from up here, Sam. Let's
just get in the water."

I focused my search around the closest areas. I saw nothing
except that whirlpool again. I wrote it off as the sharks or other fish
circling below. Chad on the other hand was still anxious to get into
the water. I tried begging him to stay out of the water, especially
since I started to discover small pieces of floating debris. I couldn't
be sure what this stuff was, but as the tide came in, I started seeing
more and more.

"Jessica, will you please speak to your boyfriend?"

"He's not my boyfriend or my responsibility, thank God."

"You slept with him, not me," I argued. In the meantime, Jesse
was close to jumping in and loved being part of our argument.

As Chad walked along the concrete pier near the back of my
boat he acted like he was losing his footing. I really didn't have
time for his bullshit game because with every passing second, I was
finding more and more debris. Chad was giggling like a girl as he
paraded around acting like he was falling in. Jessica was absolutely
no help, in fact she was laughing along with him.

"Jesse, you are not helping the situation," I pointed out angrily.

"It's funny and what do I care if he falls in?"

"You should care, he's more your friend than mine."

Having heard enough on the subject, Jessica bristled and
fired back, "It was a mistake alright … I wish it would not have
happened, but it did and I cannot change that."

Her comment was just what Chad needed to hear. He stopped
his foolishness and stepped safely on the back of the boat.

"Hey, did I hear that right? You wished it never would have
happened."

Jessica looked down to the floor as she thought of what to
say next. While that was going on and their discussion became
more heated and more private, I focused my attention on the
searchlight and what was appearing in the water. With each wave,
I was finding more and more debris. And it looked to be driftwood

from a boat wreck. It kept coming in and hitting my Dad's boat. I knew how he loved this vessel and I didn't want the responsibility of the damages. Macy was awoken by the argument between Jessica and Chad. She appeared in her long T-shirt rubbing her eyes and yawning, "What are you guys doing?"

I decided to stay out of things ... another benefit of not sleeping with Chad. The three of them tried working out their differences .... very loudly. I continued looking into the shallow water close to the dock. With my searchlight, I saw another whirlpool just off the end of the boat. With the tide coming in and bringing the fog with it, it became very still around and the boat. I heard a fish or something splash from the water. Suddenly it seemed like all of the crickets and frogs stopped making any noise, and the only noise was the water lapping against the hull of the fiberglass boat. It became very serene and then came the smell.

I wasn't the only one that noticed the strong smell. It smelled like old trench that maggots had gotten in to.

"Oh my, something smells rotten," Macy exclaimed.

I was waiting for some sort of crude sexual reference from Chad, but it never came.

"It smells like the fishermen had thrown out scraps and this thick fog is just letting it hang around.

I wouldn't go anywhere near the water now, Chad."

"Why is that Samantha?"

"Do you hear the sharks feeding?"

"No, all I hear is that foghorn blowing like every minute."

"Maybe we don't know what we are listening for," Macy pointed out and continued, "I've never been around here this early or late. It's really kind of strange."

I shone the spotlight into the open part of the water and described what was happening. They noticed the small circles on the surface and the shark fins cruising along. It was a strange sight, but I was busy watching something else. There was another one of those whirlpools just out of the range of my spotlight. I didn't say anything because they all seem a little skittish; including Chad when they saw the amount of sharks so close to the boat dock.

"Is it the sharks that smell this bad?" Jessica asked.

"My dad used to tell me that this is the time of the day when the world started over. You know, like it's just waking up. The fishermen are cutting bait, the sharks are eating and the sun is rising above the fog. My dad taught me that the fog played tricks with your mind. It distorts the sounds and visuals, but there was no denying this whirlpool was coming directly towards the back of the boat. Also thinking back to my Dad's advise, my main concern should be for my crew. They were all gathered together leaning against the rail along the back. As the whirlpool continued getting closer, I sprang into action.

"Hey guys, get away from the railing."

Of course they did not listen and I had to yell at them, as if they were children. I screamed, "Get the hell away from the railing!"

They grumbled and moaned calling me a bitch, but they did disperse just in the nick of time. The whirlpool came almost onto the boat and then suddenly we heard a splash and were horrified.

Chapter 6

As if shot from a cannon in the bottom of the harbor, a man's body landed on the back deck. Jessica screamed with surprise while the rest of us inhaled quickly. Chad was the only one able to speak immediately.

"What the….," was all he got out before we all circled the body.

"Is he dead," Macy asked?

"Not only is he dead, but severely disfigured. I wonder if somebody did this to him, or if he was in some sort of accident. His face and head looked all cut and sliced up. His right eye was bulging from the socket and it quickly became obvious where the stench we were smelling was emanating from."

"What do you think happened to him," Chad asked, now forgetting to be macho like he was before.

"I don't know, it looks like he was hit by a passing boat or something," I answered.

I saw Jesse studying the body for clues. She got a whole lot closer than either Macy or I and was acting like she had some sort of experience examining corpses. Knowing we were all watching her, she tried to explain. "I'm a big fan of CSI. Don't look at me like that … I'm just curious that's all."

40

"Well I'm radioing the Coast Guard,."

"Are you sure that's the best thing to do Samantha?"

"I'm sure Macy; it's the only thing to do."

"I'm not so sure Sam," Jessica popped off.

"What do you mean, you're not sure?"

"This looks a little like the bad guy we met at the restaurant."

"Rollings," I questioned? "Even more reason to call it in."

"Just a minute Sam," Macy said sticking up for her man, "Chad may have a point. There were a number of people who saw you guys at the bar."

"She's right and who knows how many of them saw him grab you by the arm and then he ends up dead on your boat. What is the Coast Guard going to think?"

"I don't care what they think, we didn't do anything."

Chad launched into an alternative theory of what happened.

"Picture this … four friends go out for a night of partying, - all Americans mind you," he spread his fingers apart to accentuate his points. "They have a little too much to drink and are talking with a local about a sunken treasure. Next thing you know, he winds up dead on your boat. I don't know Sam, that sounds a little hard to swallow."

"When you say it like that Chad, it makes it sound like we did something and we all know we didn't."

"Who's going to believe that a dead body shot up out of the water and landed on your boat? The specific boat that this guy has a relationship with. That's all I'm saying Macy."

Jessica stood up from kneeling beside the body and came over towards me. She put her hands on my shoulders and pointed out, "Sam, I hate to say this but those scratches around his face and his skull could be construed or mistaken for knife slashes. Of course, I'm no expert."

"Make a decision please," Macy begged as she began to vomit over the side of the boat.

Chad, the big strong hero, wants to be by his girl. I could hear him consoling her and agreeing with her that the smell was awful. Jessica moved closer and whispered, "What would it hurt to just roll him back into the water and act like this never happened?"

"That would be so disrespectful," I fired back, "and it would be a secret we would have to keep forever."

Jessica thought for a moment before speaking, obviously going through all of the options, including the scandal if you were found to be involved.

"Okay, didn't you say that there were sharks down there, guarding the treasurer or something?"

Frustrated, I replied, "Damn it, I don't even know if there is such a treasure!"

"Your dad had some of the coins in exactly like that guy did."

"So," I answered, "we don't know if it means anything at all. My dad and this guy were buddies for Christ's sake. You know my dad. He would never turn his back on his buddy, especially for money. He's got plenty."

"You think that Sam, but do you really know? I mean you just found out tonight that he did not die of a heart attack."

"What's your point, Jesse?"

"My point is you need to look at this not like he's your dad, but like you have something to gain."

"What's that?" I asked.

"That's what the police call motive, Samantha… no matter what country you are in," Chad chirped, feeling proud of himself.

I couldn't believe I was actually considering what they were saying. They did have a good point however, I snuck a peek at the lifeless, blood covered body lying on the back half of my boat. He looked like someone had murdered him with a small hatchet or a knife.

"Nobody is going to believe that he just came up out of the water and landed on my boat. If you add in the confrontation between us earlier, I could see how someone might get the wrong idea."

"I wish that my father was here. He'd know what to do," I lamented out loud.

"We need a decision captain, or we will never get that smell off the deck."

Before I made my decision, I wondered what or who had done this to Rollings. I noticed a little pruning of his skin because he had been in the water, but I couldn't look at him for too long without feeling sick to my stomach. Jessica, on the other hand, would have used a magnifying glass to inspect every inch of this corpse. I don't know how she got used to putting up with the smell, but she was on her hands and knees crawling around the body.

"He's only been in the water for a short time. I'm guessing a couple of hours."

"Thanks doctor," I joked… stalling for time.

Chad, forgetting that his girlfriend was puking over the side, went to the radio. He picked it up and pretended to radio the Coast Guard.

"This is <u>The Sammy</u>; we have just killed someone over here."

Everyone, even Macy, stopped what they were doing to cast an evil look in Chad's direction. "Maybe we should listen to him Samantha. No one would ever know except us and we won't tell."

"That's very comforting Macy, but I'm not so sure."

"We kept our mouths shut when it came to me and Chad didn't we?"

I appreciated what Jessica was saying, but the truth is something like this could hang around forever. Honestly, I don't want to be indebted to all three of these people. Not for the rest of my life, I mean I just turned 30! That's a long time to keep a secret.

"If there truly are sharks down there, that would conceal any evidence," I thought silently. But they all have to help push the body over."

"Okay, we'll do it. But everyone has to participate," I ordered. "That way if any one of us breaks the silence; we are all busted. Agreed?"

Reluctantly each one of them agreed and we each grabbed some gloves from the tackle box. I could tell that some people were putting more effort into it than others. Mostly the complaints were about how bad the body smelled. It did stink and in my humble opinion, this was the cowardly way out. Chad was the most committed. He grabbed around the torso of Rollings and rested his head against the cadaver. Macy took one arm and Jessica and I grabbed the legs.

"Now, don't make a big splash, just try and flip him over the side."

That was my advice until Jesse spoke up. "If the body is floating right in here beside us, won't that look suspicious too?"

She was absolutely correct; I mean if the Coast Guard is going to come anyway when we report the body, then what hell are we doing?

I was beginning to get a little anxious. It was still two hours before sunrise, but it will be brightening up soon.

"Anybody have any suggestions?" I asked.

Chad let the body down with a big exhale. It was almost like he was holding his breath the entire time. Macy, Jessica, and I had nothing to offer and that's when Chad took over.

"I have an idea. Why don't we just strap a weight to his foot? I mean then he will be down there until long after we're gone."

"Chad," I loudly disagreed, "that is disrespectful as hell. When he was alive, he was a friend of my father's. I would never do something like that!"

"What do you suggest, Captain?"

My dad always told me that there was a great deal of responsibility when it came to running a boat, but I never in my wildest dreams thoughts that we would be trying to get rid of a dead guy. One that we didn't even kill. I came up with the best of the logical solution.

"I think what we will do is drive the boat somewhere else and then drop him over."

It was like a brand-new idea and everyone agreed enthusiastically.

I cruised the boat quietly along the pier looking for the darkest, most secluded area. My mind was still filled with concerns and I was still wondering what was going through my head when I agreed to all this. At first, I had little emotion for concern about Rollings, but then guilt started creeping in. *"Why did you let them talk you into this?"*

I maneuvered the boat into an open area far away from the lights of the pier. I shut the engine off and quietly slid the anchor over the side. I don't know why but we were all whispering, even though there was no one in sight. I came around and joined the others as we prepared to dump the body of Rollings. Everyone grabbed their assigned positions and just as we were lifting him up, I looked into the water and saw the familiar whirlpool near the side of the boat.

"That has to be my imagination, right?"

"Okay everybody on the count of three," Chad struggled to whisper. And just like that ... it was like Rollings never existed. My head was jumbled; I didn't know how I could do that. I was never sucked in by peer pressure in my life, but I certainly had been today. Jessica noticed that I was even quieter than the others and came over to me as we pulled back into our spot. She put her arm around my shoulder and whispered, "Its okay nobody knows."

I knew it was a little crazy, but I didn't agree. Seeing that whirlpool right before dumping the body made me feel like Jessica was wrong and that someone or something knows. I just feel it in the humid air and replied to Jesse, "The ocean knows what we did."

Chapter 7

I was awoken to the bright, Caribbean sunshine the next morning. I wasn't hung over, but I did feel like last evening's antics with Rollings were unjustified and just plain wrong. I can't believe that I let them talk me into disposing of him like that. I started to wonder how those cuts had gotten all over in his face and head. I tried telling myself that they did look like stab wounds and the authorities might have thought that we did it, but that was not really any reason to not notify them. I mean, what happens now? Are we supposed to just go along like nothing has happened? I questioned how everyone else might be feeling, but I was consumed by guilt. I walked quietly into the galley where Jessica said silently staring into her coffee. It looked like she was feeling the same way as me, but when I sat down beside her, what she said didn't match her look.

I mumbled, "Morning."

"Hey, it looks like it will be another beautiful day on the island of Conger," her blue eyes glistening while she smiled.

I poured myself a mug of the life giving liquid and looked at her strangely.

"You seem awful chipper for someone that feed a man to the sharks last night."

Jessica gave me a look that normally would come from Macy. It's a look of... "What do you mean" or "I didn't do anything." Whichever look it was, it disgusted me.

"Did you forget?" I asked. "I would think that's something you would remember."

"I remember alright ... I'm just trying to put it out of my mind. Sam, you know that it was the right thing to do, don't you?"

"I'm not sure of that. Yesterday at this time we hadn't done anything, but now we have and I feel like shit. I didn't feel that way yesterday ... that's all I'm saying."

Jessica tried changing the subject slightly and asked, "What do you think could have done that to his face?"

"I don't know Jess; there are a lot of strange things in the ocean."

Our quiet, adult conversation was obnoxiously interrupted by Chad and Macy.

"Look what we've found," he gleefully yelled holding up a book of some sort.

He placed it on the counter in front of us. I could tell immediately that it was my dad's handwriting, so I asked where he found it.

"Normally when we are in that position, I am staring at her ass, you know."

"Chad, please," Macy begged rolling her eyes. "They don't want to hear about that."

"Jessica might, knowing her like I do."

"I assume that he has already told you, Samantha, what a stud he is."

"Yeah I got the play by play yesterday. Isn't it strange being around the two of them?"

"It was at first, but then I realized that normally I don't beat Jessica at anything. Chad chose me over her and knowing that gets me through the awkwardness."

Chad looked like a peacock puffing out his chest as he asked, "You guys thought I was the prize ... how cool. I'm glad that you won, Macy." And then he elbowed Jessica and whispered, "Wait until she goes shopping and I will give you a chance Jesse," he smiled and winked with his left eye. This three-person drama was too much for me and I had to put an end to it.

"Okay Chad, there is no denying that you are the biggest male stud on this boat. Now what is the book?"

Originally, he stood proudly thinking what I said was a compliment, and then he figured out that it wasn't. "Hey, I'm the only guy on this trip so of course I'm going to be the only stud." It was almost worth the wait, wiping that confident smirk off of his face, but then I realized I was the only one on this trip that he had not been to bed with and really that should have been satisfaction enough.

"Just tell them what you found," Macy ordered.

"I've found the lost journals of Jonathan," he exclaimed holding them skyward. "Did you know that your father paid for that treasure map five or eight years ago. They thought it was from some con man on the island."

"What makes you think that he was a con man?" I asked.

Chad kind of shrugged his shoulders and didn't answer.

I would believe that, if it wasn't for Rollings and these coins. That map must have shown something, or where did all this stuff come from?

"Did you read any of his journals?"

"I read one and that was all."

"Why just the one?" Jessica asked. "Did they start to get too personal?"

"Well, it made me a little sad the way he was talking about Rollings. But the truth is - once I read about him finding the treasure, I stopped, because we are parked right on top of it. It was like your old man was guarding the treasure from anyone else, by parking this boat here until you could come down. It's a brilliant plan and now with that other guy out of the way, it all ours. I am going to get my shit on right now and start diving."

Macy sternly opposed, "You are not going in there alone. Tell them what else you found out."

Chad looked down at the floor almost as if someone had stolen a birthday present from him. "Your dad wrote about a creature guarding the treasure, but it's probably not true. It's probably just a legend to keep everyone else away."

Macy looked at her pussy whipped boyfriend like he was a 10-year-old and he answered,

"Do you really believe that? I mean come on ... a 6 foot long bladed creature that eats intruders?"

"What are you talking about, Chad?"

"In your father's journals there are warnings about a killer beast that watches over the treasure, along with some sharks and personally, I happen to think its all bullshit."

Jessica, the one that had spent the most time in close proximity to the body, was of course listening in and put in her two cents. "Now that I think about it those marks all over his head and face might have been done by a large sea creature looking for something to eat, or protecting his territory."

Chad did not believe any of it and spend the next 10 minutes arguing with Jessica. I took notice of him putting on his snorkeling gear while the pair was arguing. I knew from experience that a full-blown argument was coming between Macy and Chad, but I didn't interfere, I just let it happen.

"How can people be so intimate a couple of hours ago and then turn on each other so harshly? I guess that's why I was not in a hurry to have a steady boyfriend," I thought silently, while scanning the harbor. There really wasn't a whole lot of activity, a few commercial ships and a local doing some net fishing. I watched the slender, shirtless young man throw his net repeatedly. I was watching his muscles work, with the sweat glistening off his back when I realized that I was hornier than I thought. I focused on his skill of repeating the same physical movements over and over again. The naives here had never really turned me on in the past, but I couldn't take my eyes off the young lad. I don't really know why, but I stayed behind my sunglasses watching his every move and fantasizing quietly. Around me the argument was still raging, with Macy telling Chad how stupid he was being and him arguing back about the money. I stopped listening to the argument and turned my head back to the native and his young, muscular body."

I didn't even notice the large whirlpool beside his tiny boat until it was too late. I turned my head just in time to see a large, slimy looking arm coming out of the water. Without a moment's hesitation, the arm circled around the native's waist and he was ripped from his small canoe. It happened as quickly as a flash of lightning. I couldn't hear the splash and his attempts to call for help, but they were so waterlogged I couldn't make them out. I guess that I was in shock after what I had just seen because all I can do was point and cover my mouth. Jessica was the first to notice my movements.

"What's wrong Sam?"

But I couldn't answer. I just watched in horror as the crystal blue ocean turned dark, first red then a black color. Macy and Chad took a break from their argument and turned towards me.

"What is it Samantha?" Macy asked.

Even if I could talk, I couldn't describe what I had just witnessed. The ocean along the pier was as flat as glass seconds later, when I gathered myself to speak. Chad and Macy picked up their argument right where it had stopped. What bothered me was that after their initial reaction to me …neither one of them could have cared less. Jessica was different. She disappeared inside the boat for a moment and then emerged with a glass of water.

"Are you okay Samantha?"

I took the glass of water from her and my shaking hands spilled the contents all over my lap. I scanned the harbor area looking for evidence of what I had just witnessed, but I found none. There was nothing! There was no floating body or capsized boat. There was only the reflection of the sun off of the water everywhere I looked. Jessica could tell that I was looking for something and that I was still shaken up. In a calm voice, she sat next to me and held my hand.

"You saw something, didn't you?"

"I… I was watching this young fishermen," I stated and then stopped. My eyes were nervously moving from side to side and blinking constantly. It wasn't like I was going to cry, but I knew that something emotional was about to take place.

"Okay ... so you were watching a fishermen and then what?"

Suddenly everything that I had seen came flowing out of my mouth at the same time. My explanation was so jumbled that it forced Jessica to give me a hug. She squeezed me tightly and did her best to console me.

"It's okay dear, what did you see?"

I mumbled something and held my forearm in the air. *"God Samantha, settle down and tell the story,"* I scolded myself. *"You didn't even know that kid."*

The reality is that I can't settle down. I was shaking all over, it was obvious when I tried to drink from my glass, and the water kept splashing onto my nose.

"I don't think I have ever seen you like this is Sam. Usually you are so confident and sure of yourself. I have never told you this, but I have always been envious of you."

I rolled my eyes while I took another sip of water. Jessica caught my glance and started explaining herself.

"No, I mean it," she promised. "I was always jealous of you. I mean you played volleyball, you're so pretty, and have good common sense."

While Jessica was showering me with praise, I noticed Chad slipping into the water. After what I had just seen take place, I certainly didn't want him diving. I quickly got up from my lounge chair and shouted angrily at him.

"Chad, get out of the water!"

However, he could not hear me and Macy came up onto the top deck to join us.

"I am the captain of this boat and when I tell someone something; they need to follow the directions!"

"I tried to talk him out of it but it wasn't working. Then I told them to wait on the rest of us, but he couldn't. What was I supposed to do?"

To be honest I really didn't care what she did, but I wanted Chad out of the water right now. I basically freaked out, emotionally. It must have been whenever I witnessed what happened to that young man, or what we did with Rollings. The cause didn't really matter right now as I started running to the back of the boat, screaming to Chad. Of course he couldn't hear me, but everyone else on the pier could. The sun had burned through all of the clouds and I could feel the heat of my emotions rising inside of me. I continued to give Chad hell from the boat and he continued to ignore me. I wasn't sure what I was saying and to be honest I didn't know if it was even making sense, but everyone around us knew that I was worked up into a frenzy.

"What is your problem?" Macy had the nerve to ask. "That cruise liner is starting to let people off the ship and I don't know if the locals would appreciate some crazy lady screaming her head off."

Jessica lifted up her expensive, designer sunglasses and stated the obvious as only she could. "At least she's been wearing a bikini."

After a solid two minutes of screaming at Chad and him not responding, and the other two on the boat not showing any concern, I took things into my own hands. As with any watercraft in America, The Sammy is equipped with a long, fiberglass hook to fish things out of the water. It is probably 6 feet long and the hook is not real sharp or pointy as it is made to be slipped around somebody or something to pull out of the water. I remembered were the hook was immediately, but I had only used it to fish out some clothing that had fallen overboard. I had never used it like you were supposed to.

Even though I was wearing sunglasses, it was hard see Chad due to the glare. It was also difficult because I could hear that the people on the pier talking and watching me. I had my swimsuit top and my cover-up for my bottom half, but I could still feel them watching and became self conscious. I'm sure that it made me look silly but I was having a hard time because of the refraction whenever the handle went into the water. I couldn't really tell how close I was to Chad although he was diving off the back of the boat. I tried more than half a dozen times, stabbing blindly into the water.

"Man, this is tougher than it looks. Maybe rather than trying to scoop him up I should just get his attention."

I took some shots at just jabbing at him, but he was too far down. I didn't see it at first, but just behind the boat was a whirlpool beginning to form. I panicked and started screaming his name while trying to get his attention with the hook. One nice thing about the Caribbean waters is that they are very clear. I looked in the direction of the whirlpool, but didn't see a shark or anything ... it just looked like the sandy bottom. I remembered the other time that I had seen this whirlpool of activity and it always ended the same ... in death! I continued blindly jabbing into the water, hoping and praying that I would get lucky. I thought that I saw something moving in the water in the direction of Chad, but it must have just been the glare. I hadn't heard any splashing other than Chad, but that may or may not have been true since I was so nervous. I was almost hyperventilating and considered just jumping in beside him to get his attention.

Meanwhile Macy and Jessica started taking notice of my yelling.

"Chad, get out of the water," I yelled. "Chad, God damn it, do you hear me?"

That scream brought the other girls running and soon also brought more attention from the travelers entering the pier.

"Why wouldn't it," I thought. "Three bikini clad women acting like fools."

I didn't even need to explain the exact danger to my girlfriends who now realized I was seriously panicking, so they joined into my chorus of screams to Chad.

"Give me that stick," Jessica insisted.

I did like she asked and after her second try she made contact. I was amazed until she explained that her sunglasses, all $400 of them, don't allow the refraction of the water.

"Chad, the captain wants you out of the water."

"What for, I was having a blast, you guys should try it."

"We are going to as a group, right after lunch. Now come on up here and listen to the boss."

Chad looked like a 10-year-old whose mom had just scolded him. He held his head down while Macy draped a towel over his wet head and he removed his mask.

"It's great down there. Fish were everywhere and more colorful than I have ever seen."

What's the deal anyway? I thought that we were trying to find this treasure."

"We will look for it but only after Samantha says so."

I tuned out the couple's incessant bickering and stared out into the harbor. I know what I saw this morning actually happened. It was not my imagination and what I couldn't get out of my mind was the horribly disfigured corpse of Rollings.

"Who or what could have done that? Is it possible that my father's writings were telling the truth? Is there really a gigantic, eight legged monster patrolling these waters? When I think back to what I know about the ocean; its strangeness and curiosities, maybe it's possible. I'm beginning to think that I need to read that journal."

"Do you care to let the rest of us in on what you are thinking Sam?" Jessica asked curiously.

I paused naturally for a second and then pushed my gold sunglasses on to the top of my head and said, "Let's get inside and out of the heat, and then take a good look at that journal."

Chapter 8

I started reading my father's journals with excitement. I thought that they would be all about finding the sunken treasure and what went on down there. I couldn't have been more wrong. Yeah, there were stories about the treasure, curses, and who purged it, but the majority of stories were about my mom and me. I know that people don't expect to have their private thoughts on display after they have left this earth so they are more open than usual. But some of it was downright nasty and unexpected for a proper, buttoned-down, father. He called my mom an "exacting bitch" on more than one occasion. I guess that this type of thing is common for divorced parents but I had no idea. When comparing some passages to others, I could tell when my old man was becoming intoxicated. In his mind would ramble from loving thoughts about me to hatred for my mother. In one particular passage he talks about "playing nice" to convince her to come down here for an old-fashioned family vacation. At that time, he writes; "I will show that bitch the treasure and feed her to the devilfish. That should be enough to hold her for a while and then I will go and retrieve the colons."

"Did he really feel that way about mom," I wondered silently.

Apparently he did because throughout his journal he's made references to pushing her overboard.

My eyes were drawn away from his ramblings and threats to a series of dates and numbers listed on earlier pages. Perhaps the threats and anger were just too much for me to read right now, so my eyes created a diversion. I wondered what these numbers and dates meant. Unlike some of his drunken passages, the ease entries were neat and organized, almost like the checkbook he used to keep. My other three friends were sitting below listening to the radio and looking at some of Daddy's possessions. I was getting a little nervous until Chad broke the ice.\

"Hey, I didn't know that your father smoked."

"He didn't, why?"

"Well I found this gizmo and didn't know what it was. After reading the bottom I found out that it's for rolling your own smokes."

"Duh, Rollings was his best friend. I'm sure he bought those as a gift for him. They probably spent most of their time together here, so he just left it onboard."

That got the ball rolling and then Jessica, who was doing something on her phone piped in. "Did you know that devilfish can mean two things? On one hand it can mean any fish that has a fin that resembles the devil and the other is an octopus. According to the internet where I was watching some videos, these things are pretty prevalent around the Caribbean."

"I guess it's the warm water," I added.

"It doesn't say, but come and look at these things. Aren't they freaky?"

We each tried looking at the video over Jessica's shoulder. Everyone was quiet as the announcer spoke ... just like the educational filmstrips in high school:

The octopus has the ability to change color to perfectly blend with the sea floor, or a coral reef that it's passing over. Some octopi are nomadic, but most keep a territory that they will defend violently if provoked. Along with changing colors the octopuses has many other defenses, such as its ability do dart quickly out of trouble by using a tube to propel itself. This same tube is to used to expel its famous ink to ward off predators or deliver a blinding blast to a potential food source. It grabs the food item by covering it completely with its body and then it lets its parrot like beak, which is strong enough to puncture a man's skull, do the rest."

Each of us sat in silence for different reasons. My reason was that I was horrified that my father actually had wanted to push my mom overboard and expose her to a creature like that. I think that it took some of the wind out of Chad's desire to do some snorkeling, but I could be wrong. However his next comment proved that I wasn't.

"Did he say that they love the Caribbean?"

"That's what he said," Jessica answered.

"And Jonathan Silver says that's what in regards to the treasure? We may have to rethink this, right honey?"

Macy didn't answer right away, she seemed lost in thought and until Chad pushed her shoulder. "I'm just kidding Macy, come on lighten up," he smiled.

But Macy did no such thing, instead she crossed her arms and legs in front of a in a defensive posture.

"Hey, really; let's go and get some sun. There is no reason to be huddled down here in the dark. Can't you bring those letters or what ever upstairs," Chad reasoned.

"Sure, it's getting a little stuffy down here," I answered grabbing my journal.

We circled the classic, metal stairs and emerged into the brilliant sunlight. The sky is a deeper shade of blue down here than we would ever see in NYC and after 10 a.m., the temperature starts climbing fast.

"Man, it is nice up here, no wonder you're old man loved this island. Look at all the tourists walking down the pier," Chad pointed out. "It looks like they are lining up for something."

I had seen them do that many times over the years and felt obligated to explain.

"They are lined up for their onshore excursions. You can go horseback riding, jet skiing, parasailing, or just about anything, if you have the cash. Normally they meet out here and then split up into groups for their activity. That's how my dad found that treasure map. He just blended in with the group in a walking tour. According to his journals he and Rollings were hot to find this treasure."

"Yeah, but beware of sea monsters," Chad joked waving his arms around wildly.

It was easy to tell that Macy didn't get the same laugh out of things that Chad did and she snapped at him. "Hey, you don't know what's in there; it could be dangerous. Have you even given any more thought to the young girl that I saw ripped of f the pier? Probably not! How about the guy we threw overboard last night so that we didn't have to explain things to the Coast Guard? Don't you even care?"

It was clearly obvious based on his body language that Chad really didn't give a damn. Thankfully, rather than argue his point, he slinked quietly away, which gave me time to quietly chat with Jessica and Macy.

I wanted to tell both of them what I had seen, but I really wasn't completely sure of just what it was, so I asked Macy to describe what she had seen. She made herself very small, almost as if she was cold, while telling the story. Her voice got a little quieter, like she didn't want anyone to hear. Her boyfriend was not listening at all, so that wouldn't have been the reason for her candor, so maybe she was a little bit embarrassed.

"When it was first taking place, I wasn't sure what I was seeing, but then the blood snapped me back to reality ... there was so much blood," she cried covering her face.

"It had to be that little girl. When I went back there, she was staring at the boat almost like she wanted me to see her."

"That's crazy Macy, why would she want you to watch her get killed?"

"I don't know Jesse, I'm just telling you how it felt at the time. Do you want me to continue or not?"

Jesse quickly apologized, "I'm sorry, please continue."

"I really didn't know what happened, I mean one minute the little girl was there and the next minute there was this volcano of blood and just as quickly, it was all over. A shark couldn't have gotten her, there's no way. She was walked way too far on the land, or the pier, I mean."

I could see that just sharing the story was hard for Macy. She breathed deeply to hold back any signs of emotion and touched her fingers to her I eyes repeatedly. I am a little tougher than that, but that's not surprising, Macy has always been a drama queen, hungry for the spotlight. Jessica was being the interrogating police officer in the matter, posing questions to her as if she had killed the little girl. I tried playing peacemaker with a twist. From behind my dark sunglasses, I angrily asked, "If you saw that, why not tell me?"

"Who are you that I should tell," she snapped back with her best New York City accent.

"For one I'm your captain and tour guide, but most of all, I'm your friend."

Macy looked directly at the floor of the boat and sheepishly apologized.

"I wasn't sure that you guys would believe me … Chad never does."

When she mentioned her boyfriend, it alerted me to something, but he wasn't around. I looked over the side and was surprised to see him in the water.

"Chad," I shouted, "What are you doing?" But this guy was oblivious. He was snorkeling and diving right near the coral reef, not far from the incident that Macy was telling us about. I had a mind to just let him go, but I figured that wouldn't be very nice to my friend.

"Hey Macy, look at Chad," I pointed out.

"That jackass! I told you he didn't believe me and now he's swimming right where that girl was taken." She started yelling with my help, but it was no use.

"This is the second time that I tried to get his attention, is he that much of a dick?"

"Yeah maybe, but that's not why he can't hear you. He wears earplugs whenever he swims because he doesn't like getting water in his ears. It always gives him a cold, no matter what time of year."

"That's a pain in the ass," Jessica offered up. "How do we get his attention?"

"I'll just wait until he gets closer and then I will jump in."

We slowly meandered back down the stairs to the lower deck. It was covered by a white hard plastic canopy about 10 inches thick. I thought that was the only thing that my parents disagreed on as to whether or not the boat needed a canopy. My mother didn't want one, so she would always be exposed to the sun. My father argued that it was a fishing boat and he needed the coverage. *"Thinking back to that time and finding his journals showed me that they argued about a hell of a lot more than that."*

The boat itself is extremely fast with dual inboard motors, not just for quickly getting from fishing spot to fishing spot, but part of the deal when my dad purchased it was to go island hopping in the Caribbean. The boat has a cutaway and a head, both terms my father taught me, as well as GPS navigation which was upgraded with a flat screen a couple years ago. I thought back fondly to the times that just the two of us are out here. He really enjoyed teaching someone how to handle this boat. My mother had no interest in learning and maybe it is what pissed off my father so much. He felt like a deckhand on his own boat. I thought back to mother ordering him around and he just took it. I wish that I would have been around during my teenage years to kind of stick up for the guy. He always just smiled and I never heard them argue.

"I guess that it's true that it takes two to have an argument. I can remember asking him about it once and he smiled that broad dead smile, messed up my hair and explained," I argue with people all day everyday Sammy and I don't want to do it here. This place is special, you're special, and that's why I named the boat after you."

It wasn't just what he said... it was the sparkle in his eyes when he said it. The two of us shared many special moments over the years, but my love for this boat and learning everything from how to start it, too ocean safety rules and regulations is something that I will never forget. Something else that I will never forget was him telling me some of the local legends. I think it all started when he gave me that first coin. I can remember it like yesterday. There was more fire in his eyes then I had ever seen and I remember thinking that this must be how he is when it comes to a business deal. He told me about the map and then finding the actual treasure while diving with Rollings. He explained that they had only been able to bring small amounts to the surface because of the sharks and devilfish which were guarding the treasure. I didn't really believe him, I'm ashamed to say, but maybe something it is actually out there. It would explain what Macy saw and maybe even what I saw.

My attention was drawn below by a large cannonball splash as Macy jumped into the water. I noticed that Jessica looked a little somber, so I edged closer to her.

"Why are you so quiet," I asked sounding concerned.

She shrugged her shoulders and looked a little afraid while meekly answering, "Have you looked through all of these journals?"

"I have glanced at them, but I haven't really studied them. Why?"

For some reason she looked terrified watching Macy and Chad frolicked above the reef in the shallows, somewhat like an overbearing parent.

"We shouldn't stay here. We need to weigh anchor and get away from around here."

"Don't be silly Jesse … this place has everything. It has shops, bars, restaurants, and a new group of attractive men every week. Why should we go anywhere? Oh yeah, and it's got a treasure beneath of us."

Her blue eyes looked almost white with fear as they nervously switched back and forth from the frolicking couple back to me. "What in the world is wrong," I asked, you look pale as hell?"

"I don't know, I just have the feeling that something's wrong."

I was just about to explain how ridiculous she was acting and then I heard the scream. It was high pitched and piercing and I knew it came from Macy. Both Jessica and I rushed to the back of the boat. Macy was actually standing on a small sandbar slapping it the clear, blue waters screaming, "Get away! Leave him alone!"

That's when I saw it for the first time. It is huge and wrapped entirely around Chad.

"Oh my God," was the only comment that I could muster. I really couldn't tell what had hold of him, but it looked like some sort of eel or something. I remembered thinking how scarlet in color this thing appeared. It looked like the devil himself! Chad was struggling as hard as he could, with his arms flailing around everywhere and gasping for breath.

I yelled to Macy. "Do you have your knife? You need to stab that thing, to make it let go." She either didn't understand or wasn't able to hear me over the struggle going on between Chad and this monster. For a moment I watched as this thing tried to push Chad under. And then I realized what was going on, from reading my dad's journals.

"This is the devilfish that guards the treasure, he must have gotten too close to it," I thought.

It is the first time that I have ever seen one of these 'things'. It did not look like the short film that we launched moments earlier. This thing had two black eyes and a huge cone shaped head. Macy continued screaming, which wasn't doing anything to help her boyfriend. Each time it seemed like the thing was holding him under longer.

"Don't let him cover your head," Jesse yelled, "that's what he is trying to do. He wants to put you under there so that he can eat you!"

"I had never heard of any man eating octopus, but what ever, she is the one that studied the movie."

I was more concerned that he would not be able to breathe. I saw Jessica get up and get the long hook. Chad and this creature were battling off the rear end of the boat, just far enough away that Jessica could not get much leverage on the large life-saving equipment. I went beside her and tried to assist. It was hard but after a couple of tries, we figured out a system. We extended the rod to its maximum length and despite her screams we were able to jab at the creature. It was wrapped around him like a boa constrictor, taking him under the water for a longer and longer period each time. We managed to whack him on four consecutive tries, and we've put a little more behind each one. The animal was pushing Chad under and trying to get a better hold of him. Macy's screams of fear had turned into cheers for our efforts. We continued swinging away, until hitting it square on its large head, and as quickly as it had began, it stopped and let Chad go. The three of us girls, as you well as Chad, were terrified and looked over our shoulders to see if it swam away or if was still lurking below our sight.

Chad didn't appear to know where to go ... he appeared dazed and disoriented. I was thankful that he was alive. He threw up some salt water and Macy walked to the sandbar to his side. I had never seen anything like this happen live. It was horrible ....horrible!!! I thought back to my fathers journals and was curious what Chad had done to provoke this beast. We helped him onto the ladder hanging on the rear of the boat.

"Is he okay," Macy asked over and over.

He appeared fine. He had no cuts on him, but some bruises where the monster's head wrapped around him. To be on the safe side I radioed the shore. We are parked in the harbor, so we could get him to a hospital if needed. I didn't feel that we needed the Coast Guard, or water patrol, which is what they call it down here. I wasn't sure if the quickest thing would be to take him via boat or have someone meet us on the pier. That's why I was radioing in. My transmission was scratchy at best. I fiddled with each of the knobs, trying to get better reception. Macy was hugging Chad with her back to the open sea. Jessica was doing her best to calm her down, but Macy wasn't listening. From my spot near the driver's area, I could hear the chatter between the two old friends. They weren't really arguing, it was more like Jessica channeling Macy as to how to behave and trying to convince her everything was alright.

Rather than be appreciative, Macy insisted that things were not okay. While the two discussed things, I focused on the radio, which was not working. I quickly checked the connections and to me everything looked fine, but I guess something was crossed some place. I grabbed the first aid kit and cleared off the table for Chad to lay on.

"Come over here," I yelled towards the back of the boat. "I've got a makeshift operating table all set up."

However, the group seemed to lack a sense of urgency and seemed disinterested in what I had been doing up front. When I looked back, they seemed to be acting like everything was fine. Macy was still standing on the sandbar, blue water up to her navel and Jessica was looking after Chad. She was rubbing his shoulders as he lay on the deck composing himself. The radio was still not working and they looked like they were on vacation. There were smiles and laughs from everyone and it looked to me like Macy was describing the events to Chad. He reached for a towel to wipe his face and head and I thought, is he really drying his hands so that he could light up a smoke. Jessica came into the galley and noticed the table.

"What is all of this," she asked?

"It was going to be my work area, if I needed it," I answered. "I can't get that radio to work and I was hoping to call for help."

"I don't think we'll have to worry about him. He's back there having a smoke and I just came up for the ash tray. Wait till you see what Chad found. He always likes his swim trunks to have pockets and he has them filled with more than a dozen of those gold coins from the bottom of the ocean."

I picked up one of the silver dollar sized coins off of the drivers console and held it out.

"You mean one of these?"

"Yeah, just like that, the same lady on the front and everything. He said that he gave a couple to Macy to hold while he recovered."

"Jesse, have you ever seen anything like that? I mean that sea creature was really going after him."

"It's a good thing he is a strong swimmer."

Jessica agreed and started walking towards the back of the boat without answering my question. She looked over her shoulder while she was walking away and shouted, "No I have never heard of octopi being territorial except during mating season and I certainly have never heard of one guarding a treasure and eating a man."

"Yes she had. Rollings told us that it's what killed my father. Maybe she was too out of it to remember, or maybe since it wasn't about her, she wasn't listening."

I guess that was a little bitchy of me to think like that. Jessica has really been great during our trip ... better than she had ever been in the past. Normally, she wouldn't help with things, but so far she has been pulling her own weight with things like cooking and laundry, not just expecting to pick up the check. Inside I've felt guilty and was going to sit with her and talk, selfishly to make myself feel better. I looked for my dad's Journal before I went outside. That's when it happened.

I was alerted by the scream and turned around quickly. I didn't see anything at first and then I realized that Macy was no longer standing near the back.

"Macy, hang on ... I'll save you," Chad shouted immediately diving in.

Jesse looked in shock and was frozen like a statue. This time the creature did not wrestle with its prey. It took Macy completely under the water. She's not as big as Chad and definitely not as strong. There is no way she could stay under the water that long. Chad surfaced and frantically whipped his head around.

"Where is she ... damn it!"

He took a large breath of air and dove down to look again. To be honest, I froze as well and I don't know why. I am the best swimmer of the group and the one in charge and I just stood there watching like a chump., From my vantage point above I could even see Macy is struggling with what looked to be an enormous octopus. The animal was able to drag his long legs over her head and it surprisingly covered her entire body.

"What am I watching? Why don't you help her?"

But I couldn't! I didn't! I just stood there watching my friend struggling inside the grips of this evil. I would say that it was the same devilfish that had hold of Chad moments earlier, but I couldn't be sure. I didn't think there would be two of them that size, but maybe. Macy was under the water for a long time and I watched as the animal shut its long reddish colored legs around her body. It spammed and pulsated back and forth very quickly and then the crystal clear water turned red with blood and the struggle was over.

Chad climbed onto the boat sucking air. He laid flat on the deck crying, "Did you see that? I couldn't get to her. He took her too deep. Do you think she's gone?"

There is no doubt in my mind. Rather than answer, I picked him up with Jessica's help and placed him in one of the chairs.

"What am I going to do?" he cried with more emotion than I ever thought I would see from him.

"It'll be okay," we assured him. But that was a bold face lie! I don't think that I will ever be okay after what I saw. I was replaying the events in my head over and over, trying to think of what I could have done to save my friend. It was a helpless and empty feeling because I came up with nothing. But as the captain of this boat and that person responsible for the other three lives left, I had to come up with something. Even if it doesn't work it's better than doing what I did, which is standing there watching my friend get killed. The more that I thought about what I had seen; the more nauseated I became and had to vomit into the water over the side of the boat.

Chapter 9

My mind is swirling, just like the whirlpool that I keep seeing over and over. I have just lost one of my best friends, right before my eyes. I don't think that I will ever be able to get the gruesome, bloody water out of my mind.

"This as supposed to be a fun trip. You know, three old friends from NYC drinking, sunning and cruising around the Caribbean. I was planning on some dirty dancing with a few hot Latino men, but now that was the furthest thing on my mind. I'll be lucky to get me out of here alive.

I had a knot in my gut telling me ... hell it was begging me ... to call the authorities and just go home. I certainly wasn't thinking straight after being involved peripherally in two deaths in the last 24 hours. I stumbled to the radio to call in about Macy. My hands were shaking so badly that I had to turn to Jessica for assistance with the microphone.

"Can you help me," I asked flatly still in a state of shock.

"What do I say?"

"Get in contact with somebody and I'll do the talking."

I can see the surprised look on her face as I walked away, looking into the ocean. I let them talk me into something I was uncomfortable with when it came to discarding Rollings body. I made the decision right then that I was never feel compromised again. Reading what I did of my dad's journals told me a little about taking charge and being a captain.

"So far I have failed at both being a captain, but more importantly being a friend," I thought to myself.

Things had to change and change quickly. Chad was sitting cross-legged on the deck sucking down one of his smokes. I'm not really sure what prompted me, but I asked if he had given any of the coins to Macy.

"Yeah, four or five of them."

"This is going to sound strange, but did the octopus know that?"

"I'm not sure what he knew, Sam. I was wrestling with him and all I can remember is an he took Macy, and now she's gone. What am I going to do?"

"Chad, I really need to be focused right now. I loved Macy too ... the three of us have been best friends since, it doesn't matter. I loved her. How many coins did you take?"

Chad pulled out his pockets to reveal a couple more of the gold coins. He looked puzzled and a little stunned, which prompted me to ask what was wrong.

"I had 30 or 40 coins that I had gathered this morning, but now after that wrestling match with that, that thing out there, I don't have many left."

"That's exactly what I thought. That thing, whatever it is, is guarding the treasure. I need some more information. Chad, do you feel up to reading some more of the journal that you found?"

"What are we going to do about Macy?"

"I'll find out what is happening with the radio, but I promise we'll get it reported to the authorities."

I slipped by Chad, who was doing what I asked. to check in on Jess. She looked frustrated with the radio and that was confirmed by her statement when I closed in on her. "I can't get anything on this damned radio!"

"I couldn't either. There is a local police station at the other end of the pier."

"How is Chad?"

"He needs us right now, especially you. Why don't you help him go through the journals and I will drive us to the other end of the pier to the station. Sit down and hold on."

"I thought that you were not supposed to speed in the harbor."

"I'm not, but what is the worst thing that can happen; we are already going to the police."

Jessica just nodded her head while moving to a seat beside Chad. I waited until they were settled and then I un-tied the boat from the weathered, wooden dock. The harbor is full of cruise goers parasailing, horseback riding along the beach and any other activity you can imagine. I stopped looking towards the island and unleashed Sammy with her full power. There was a group on a waterman sailboat, sight seeing and doing their best to get in my way. I needed to get around this group quickly, so once again I cranked up the inboard motor. I went around them with the front of Sammy sticking up out of the water like I was riding on the back wheel of a motorcycle and that's when I saw the patrol. It's blue light affixed to the top of the white patrol boat immediately began flashing.

"I knew that I was busted, but it really that was probably the easiest way to get police involved."

As soon as I caught the flash of the blue light out of my right eye I slowed down. There really wasn't any place to pull over, but the officer appreciated what I had done. He threw over a line and Jessica tied us together. The good-looking Jamaican, wearing a white shirt and khaki pants boarded my boat. He is about my height, slender, with a completely shaved head, wearing black Wayfarer sunglasses. His accent was unmistakable the minute he spoke. I could almost hear the reggae music playing as he climbed aboard, putting the sunglasses up on the top of his heady asking, "What's the rush?"

I didn't want to sound like a flake, or some scared girl ... which truly I was. I took a couple of deep breaths and answered proudly, "My radio is not working properly sir and we have had a terrible accident."

As he scanned the interior of the boat, he smiled again. "Everything looks fine to me. Who is it that has the story about an accident?"

In my mind I knew what the cop would think if I'd just blurted out what had happened. I could just see his eyes when I told him that my friend was killed by a giant octopus who is guarding a lost treasure ... so I explained it a different way.

"One of our crew went overboard and never came back up."

"Exactly where did this happen?" the officer asked sounding concerned, but not really surprised.

"I expect that happens frequently, with all of the drinking and inexperienced boaters that are around. However, I wasn't going to say that to him."

"Have you been drinking today?"

I kept my cool even though inside I was fuming. I was offended that this was the first thing anyone would think of, but it's probably true. I answered his routine questions and he told me to point out the area where Macy fell overboard. I showed him where we were docked and he had a strange look on his face. Then after a few moments of silence and staring out into the sea longingly, he finally spoke. "You must be careful in this harbor. It's very busy and gets a little choppy, which tends to throw people overboard. It's happened before and will no doubt happen again."

"Well that certainly wasn't the explanation I thought it would be. There's something about this guy, he knows something."

I stared into the water, ignoring the people who were having the time of their life enjoying this beautiful ocean spot. The reflection of the sun caused me to squint and put my hand over my eyes as a shield. I really don't know what I was looking for. Maybe in some gruesome way, I wanted Macy to surface while the cop was there with me. Or maybe the body of Rollings floats up. I don't know, but I thought that if we were together when either of these events happened, I could find out what the hell was going on in this harbor. Jessica and Chad said quietly only giving the officer a brief wave hello. I was thinking that Chad would just start spilling everything, but to this point, he hadn't.

No sooner did I think that, when Chad stood up and cleared his throat. "Excuse me officer," he began.

"Just keep your mouth shut Chad," I thought, "he's almost finished."

"Yeah, what is it son?"

"Do you believe in the karma from the sea?"

Jessica and I looked at him with our mouths agape. Why would he ask a stranger a question like that unless we have something to hide ... which of course we do. I couldn't help wondering what the patrol man thought.

"I have been on this island for half my life. My family moved here from Jamaica. They wanted to get away from the crime and the drugs. This was supposed to be a simpler place to raise a family, but there are worse things going on than drugs and something you call karma. Here is a missing person form, fill it out and we will do our best to look for your friend. Here is my card. Next time when you need the police, do me a favor and call me rather than speed. I would also caution you to move from where you are docked. I am sorry about your friend. Please drive safely and enjoy Conger. Hope to see you again."

I watched his boat pull away and couldn't help but think he knew more than he was sharing. I passed the form to Chad and he looked up at me with tears in his eyes.

"I ... I guess it is real now. Jessica, can I borrow your phone, my reception is lousy. I would like to call her parents."

Jesse gave him her phone and some privacy as we slowly drove back to our dock. She came to the front of the boat with me and Chad stayed in the back, having the miserable task of calling her parents. I probably should have been the one to do it, but for some reason her parents never seemed to like me ... well, not as much as they seem to like Chad. The two of us began whispering to each other as we were our way slowly back to our spot. It was hard navigating because of all the other boat traffic. The cruisers, as I like to call them, were everywhere doing activities again. It broke my heart to see the long faces on my crew compared to these travelers. Unlike the cruisers, we not only felt sorry for Chad and of course, Macy, but for ourselves.

I cast a somber gaze at Jessica and watched Chad telling Macy's parents that she was gone.

"A far cry from last night don't you agree?"

I looked at Jessica with a little surprise in my eyes. "Was my party just last night? What a screwed up last 12 hours and such a horribly sad time span."

I thought about that statement, and losing Macy, but I couldn't help but think about Rollings and the other fishermen that were killed. If there truly is something guarding that treasure, it's obvious that someone or some thing has pissed it off. To figure out how to deal with it, and just what it is we are dealing with, I will need Jessica to do some specific research.

"Have you ever seen Chad this way, Sam?"

I looked back at him, sitting on the back seat crying, talking with his hands and wiping his eyes as tears roll down his sun burnt cheeks.

"No, but I know how he's feeling. He wasn't the only one that loved her. I mean it was a while ago, and just that one time. We'd been friends forever, and we were drunk and I don't know ... I guess I was curious."

"What," Jesse exclaimed loudly causing me to lose focus and strike one of the wooden posts in the harbor, right next to where we were going to park. Everyone lurched forward suddenly and thankfully Chad didn't drop the phone into the water, but I could to see the surprise on Jessica's face. She looked almost as surprised and disgusted as I was for damaging the boat.

"Did this happen while we were all living together," she asked sternly, with her hands on her hips.

"Well yeah," I answered casually. "I can't believe that she never said anything to you."

"No, never, I mean I had no idea."

I couldn't tell if Jessica was upset because I had now confided in her, or if she was jealous that I did not choose her, so I just blurted out, "It wasn't like we were trying to keep it from you, it just happened. I figured you already knew."

Chad heard us talking about something and that's when he came up to the front of the boat. His face was wrinkled with worry and I could tell it was more the just his feelings about losing Macy.

"Um, do you realize that there is a hole in the front of the boat?"

Chapter 10

To be honest, I didn't. I was more concerned with Jessica and her reaction than anything else. Maybe I was just a little embarrassed. I had never dreamed of doing anything like that, but it just happened. I think Macy was embarrassed by it too. Only because she didn't share that with Jessica and the two of us never talked about it either. Maybe it's because we always thought that we would have time to talk about it and now she's gone. At precisely that moment, the reality of her death set in and became real.

"Oh my God," I exclaimed to myself, Macy is dead because I didn't look out for her. Everyone on this boat is my responsibility and I have failed miserably."

I needed to keep it together and get my priorities straight. We came down here for a little fun, which we have had ... now we have to get out of here before it's too late. I went up around the side of the boat to check on the damage to the bow. It was worse than I had thought. There was a 2' x 1' gash in the fiberglass. Right now it was out of the water, but when the tide comes in who knows.

Chad instinctively had to make a wise ass comment. "You hit the only thing around for about 400 yards. You should be proud of what a great captain you are."

"She didn't do it on purpose! It was my fault, I made her jump."

I really didn't think that arguing, or dissension while everyone is still a little on edge from what happened to Macy, was going to help anything.

"Guys, we are all upset," I urged them. "It's no reason to be mean to each other. We have another problem staring us in the face right now. Chad, I need you to go below and see what kind of repair stuff we have. I'd like to patch that hole if we can and get us to the island."

Chad quickly left to see what he could find below while Jessica and I stayed above near the drivers console.

"Jesse, I'm really sorry you had to find out this way."

"Don't worry about it; maybe I was just being jealous. I don't know, we all loved her in different ways and now that she's gone. It's nice to have memories. Oh shit, she's really gone, isn't she?"

Jessica could not hold her emotions back any longer and I held her and joined her in sorrow. I'm not sure what I was feeling guiltier about, was it letting my friend die or wasting time trying to find this stupid treasure? I certainly wasn't concerned about the boat enough, but maybe I should have been as *The Sammy* was taking on a little bit of water.

"Sam, I couldn't find any patching materials down there. Maybe I'm not looking in the right place."

Jessica, still in her emotional state, approached Chad and to my surprise smacked him in the face.

"Hey, what the hell," he asked.

"I'm sorry Chad, but I've promised Macy that after she was gone I would do that for sleeping with me."

"Unfortunately she is gone from us now, but you didn't need to hit me that hard."

And then the two former lovers and friends for as long as I can remember broke down in each other's clasp. I didn't want to interrupt, so I went down below to look at the repair materials myself. I was shocked to find that my normally over prepared father really didn't have a whole lot of repair materials. I started nosing around a little more and found that there are a lot of things out of order. For example, his emergency kit had been rummaged through and I could tell some items were missing. It may have been five years or so since I've been on this boat, but the things that were missing, like cotton swabs, band aids, and a fire extinguisher, where things my old man would never be without. I can still hear Chad and Jessica crying and moaning to one another while continuing to look for other supplies. However to my amazement, there were none. There was nothing that I could use to patch the rip.

I went back upstairs to break the bad news to Chad and Jessica. When I got up there, they were still holding each other and commiserating.

"I really hate to break things up, but I can't find anything to fix that hole, so I think it's best if we just have it repaired some place."

Sounding like five-year-olds the pair begged me not to make them leave.

"Do we have to, you know leave?"

"I would think that you of all people would want to get out of here Chad."

"That's just it Sam, we don't think that either one of us is ready to leave. We were talking and who knows what she would have wanted."

I couldn't believe it! There has to be more to this story than they are sharing. I wanted to ask them, but my attention was drawn to the front of the boat. Not because of the rip in the fiberglass which needed fixed, but because I saw that eerie swirling again. It was just off of the port side, near the front of the boat. The glare off of the water made it difficult to see what was causing the whirlpool. I stood and then crouched trying to avoid the reflection, but it was no use.

"Hey guys," I asked motioning for them to come here. "Can you see what is making those rings?"

Jessica, wearing her expensive sunglasses, looked for a moment and concluded, "It just looks like the reef. I mean it is exactly the same color and it's not really moving."

"Yeah, Sam maybe it was a large fish or something that jumped. I mean a lot of people fish this area, so there must be some big ones in here."

I just nodded my head in agreement, but I really didn't believe them. I kept my eyes transfixed on the spot, the dark spot of the reef while I asked, "Why don't you guys want to leave? I think it would be best with that hole in the front of the boat."

"We just don't think Macy would want us to just yet."

"Why not," I asked Jessica, "are you communicating with her from the grave in this harbor?"

I guess that my question was a little harsh and Chad and Jessica jumped on me with both feet. "She was killed, not by falling over, as you suggested to the patrolman, but by some thing in the water. Don't you want to find out what that something is? Don't you think we owe that to her Sam?"

I agreed with that, but it gave me a very uneasy feeling in the pit of my stomach.

"That's why we don't want to leave just yet. There is no body to take home, no answers to give her parents, and I felt like a buffoon talking with them. I didn't have any answers and they were just nailing me with questions. Of course, this news like that, I can't blame them at all. Her old man never liked me anyway ... now he hates me."

I heard Chad talking, but I wasn't listening. It was just like background noise as I saw more swirling on top of the water. Quickly I thought I saw something moving away from the boat. It was certainly the same color as the reef below, but it appeared to have legs, or arms and trailing behind was its huge head. The Caribbean water and is so clear that I was positive it was not just the reef. I stood up again and interrupted Chad, "There it goes!"

The pair looked at me like I was nuts. "What are you talking about Samantha?"

"Bring your phone and follow me ... there is something we need to look at in my Dad's journals." Reluctantly, they eventually follow me down the spiral metal staircase to the bowels of the boat.

Chapter 11

I didn't know exactly how to cover this topic, but between Rollings information about my father, his journals, and the feeling I got from the police, there was something different going on. I thought it was about time to share with them the two incidents that I was trying to convince myself that I didn't believe. Once below, each of us got comfortable around the high table. I had Chad open my Dad's Journal to the day before he died.

"What does Jonathan say on that day?"

With raised eyebrows Jessica tilted her head and asked, "Are you sure Sam?"

"There is a point to this, I promise. Now let me read it to you, please."

"*I feel that I am being betrayed, not by my friend Rollings, but by my mind itself. Would God create a creature such as this? Certainly it has to do with protecting the riches. I've seen them and they are numerous and spectacular ... the type of riches that could set a man and his family up for generations. I have tried to combat the beast that guards the treasure, but with its two large eyes following me everywhere, it's suction cups and its long arms I fear I will not win the battle.*"

"That sounds pretty creepy Sam."

"I agree with her, Samantha. It sounds like your old man had too much rum."

"He talks about some horrible creature guarding the treasure. Don't you see? That is what got Macy. It's what killed my father, and it's what tried to kill you Chad! I saw it kill a fisherman this morning. It's probably what Macy saw that took the little girl off of the dock. Don't you see ... it's because of these coins," I said dropping seven or eight of them onto the table.

I could tell by their expressions that they are very skeptical of what I just told them and looked at me like I was crazy. "You're telling me that you witnessed someone being killed by this thing?"

"I think so, Jesse."

"What did this as sea monster look like?"

"I only saw one of its arms. It appeared from the water and just wrapped around that fisherman and drug him into the water; just like it was trying to do to Chad and did to Macy."

Lighting up a cigarette and asking me with a wry smile, "Are you saying that I need to call back her parents and tell them that she was killed by a sea monster? We don't have any proof. Can you imagine what they would think of me? I'm going outside to think and watch the sunset as if Macy was still around. I don't believe what you are thinking. Maybe your father gave this fairy tale to you, kind of an inherited trait." Chad left in kind of a huff, leaving Jessica and I alone down below.

"Was it something I said?"

"I don't think so, Sam. I think that he just needs some time alone, to deal with all this.

"I understand, but do you see my point Jesse?"

Jessica sat there for a moment and looked back through my Dad's journals quickly.

She put her fist under her chin and pulled back her thick blond hair. Not only was she rich, but there are very few ladies that are more attractive with their hair drastically pulled back like that. She was! She sighed a heavy sigh and let her long locks tumble from her grasp.

"Okay, let's say, for the sake of argument, that there is a sea monster, or what ever. What is that monster doing with the bodies of that little girl, Macy, Rollings, and everyone else? I haven't seen anything on the internet or nature shows that say this type of monster actually eats people."

I looked at her rather angrily and thought, *"They don't talk about it being 6 foot tall either; but this one is, I've seen it."*

I began to think that Jessica was skeptical of everything that has been going on, so I asked her. "You don't believe any of this, do you?"

"I'm sorry Samantha, just look at this."

She typed something into her phone and a laid it down in front of us for viewing.

"The stories of sea monsters rising from the depths to bring down a vessel or its crew are just that, stories. The octopus is one of the friendliest sea creatures out there. It feeds on crustaceans, clams, and other hard shelled invertebrates living around a coral reef. On a few occasions, it has attacked man, but only in self-defense."

"See Samantha, that is why I have such a hard time believing you. I mean, I haven't seen anything. Not even the swirling that you keep talking about. It makes sense that there could be octopi living around this area. It supposedly is an area that has a shipwreck, which would bring in the ocean life."

Now I realized that I needed to think of a different angle. I know Jessica, she is the nicest person, but when her mind is made up, she digs in her heels. I needed something else to get are thinking. It took a moment, but I remembered Rollings and what he showed me at the bar.

"Look up my father's death certificate."

"Sam, are you sure? We already went down that road with his friend and it says <u>unknown </u>as the cause of death."

I knew that it wasn't a heart attack, like I had always been led to believe by my mother, but something struck me as odd when I was talking with Rollings.

"Okay," Jessica stated, "It says here that the deceased died of unknown causes related to most likely to a boating accident or scuba mishap."

"Did it say where he was found?"

"Sam, you already knows this, why do you want to relive it? He was found right under this dock."

"It doesn't sound like a very thorough investigation does it?" I argued.

"What do you want it to say, Samantha? I mean there is no police report here."

"I know that Jesse, that's my point! They didn't dig deep enough. I mean what were all those cuts on my father's head and face. And that cop today, he knows something."

"Why do you think that Samantha?"

"It's just a feeling that I have. Let's walk through it. If I lived in a place that relied on tourism, don't you think I would do everything in my power to cover up a marine monster?"

"Now you are just being silly."

"Am I? How many other unexplained deaths are there on this island in the last five years? And another thing, couldn't those marks have been caused by that beak on a large octopus?"

Jessica did not get a chance to answer. The two of us were standing in the middle of the galley and all of the sudden the boat rocked drastically to one side. I heard a yell which I assumed was Chad and we rushed up the stairs to see what was happening. By the time we got up there, we couldn't see anything. The darkness completely engulfed the boat. I guess Chad had turned off the outside light, either to take a nap or to be alone with his thoughts. I quickly turned the light back on to help us maneuver and look for our friend, but he was nowhere to be seen. We yelled his name over and over, "Chad, Chad are you out here?" PLEASE ANSWER!!!!

"This isn't the best time to go swimming dumb ass," Jessica yelled with panic in her voice.

I noticed a cigarette butt floating in the water next to the ladder. It was not like Chad to leave a cigarette with some tobacco left. Jessica came to join me near the very end of the boat and almost fell on the wet surface. I had to reach out and grab her.

"It's all wet back here… you don't think he jumped overboard do you?"

I knew that he was upset about Macy, but he know about the dangers in the water earlier.

"I don't think he would have gone for a swim Jesse, he was down there before and knows the dangers, especially at night."

"Don't you have one of those underwater lights on the bottom of this boat?" I was impressed with her memory and asked her to keep calling for him which she did as I went to the controls near the steering wheel. I was shaking and nearly lost my balance climbing to the command seat. Jessica was yelling for Chad and at Chad and I'm sure it could be heard everywhere around the harbor, because it was the only sound. The air was cool and a slight mist began falling as I hit the switch for the underwater light. I couldn't believe my eyes! Well actually I could, but I hadn't seen it before as clearly. In the dark blue water underneath us was a <u>huge sea monster</u> ... I mean probably 6 feet from its large round head to the end of one of its arms, dragging Chad behind it through the harbor.

"I don't believe it," I whispered to myself. Dad you were telling the truth. This harbor is cursed. I knew from that moment on that we would have to stay away from the edge of the boat."

Almost in a state of shock, Jessica gasped and stood like a statue with one of her hands covering her mouth. "Did you see the size of that thing? It's enormous."

I shook my head yes and resisted the opportunity to say to her that I told her so. Instead I waited for her next question, but I could tell was on the tip of her tongue. "What do we do now?"

I stood silently weighing our options. I could hear the bell of a distant dingy breaking the silence. The mist had subsided, but it seemed as if the darkness had gotten blacker. I switched off the underwater light, which made it that much darker. I stood tall, stoic, staring into the water that had taken my friends and my father. I needed a plan, but right now I needed to make sure that Jesse was okay. I really didn't know what I was going to but one thing is for sure, I was not about to give up.

Through her panting and with a faint breath, Jessica managed to put a few words together. "We're going in now ... aren't we? We can't be out here with that thing," she cautioned.

"Let's go below, we need a plan."

"Yeah, but we're going in right?"

I didn't answer her the second time; I just repeated the same thing. "Let's go below, we need a plan."

Chapter 12

J essica did not look like she was in a planning mood, but too bad. We needed to find out all we could about this thing, either from Dad's journals, the internet, or local legend. She followed me down the spiral staircase and had a strange, concerned look on her face. I really wasn't listening to her babble until she started describing what she had just seen.

"Did you see that thing dragging Chad away," she asked frantically while joining me below. "It had long tentacles that were wrapped around Chad's head."

I was in survival mode and I really wasn't sensitive to her feelings when I fired back, "I think those were his brains. Octopi, as you call them, do not have tentacles."

After a loud "Ewww" Jessica sat down next to me. She seemed to be trying to get over her fears pretty quickly, which worked well for me since we had a serious job to do.

"Put that out of your mind Jesse. If you don't, we might both end up like him."

Jessica blew away the strains of blond hair hanging in front of her blue eyes and put her elbows onto the table and asked, "What can I do?"

"Now that's the spirit I was looking for and needing. I might have been coming off like I didn't care about Chad. But that's not true; I can't imagine what he or Macy had to endure while they struggled for their lives. I can almost feel the tightening of the large creature's grip around my neck, cutting off the blood flow. If they were lucky, perhaps they blacked out before getting their skull punctured."

"That's the Jessica that I know," I encouraged. "This radio sucks, so maybe I could borrow your phone. I want to call that harbor patrol officer and see what he knows; I have a feeling he was holding something back."

"What do you want me to do?"

"Since I'll have your phone and we can't find out anymore until I'm done, I need you to go through these journals and find anything that you can about the treasure and that thing guarding it. I'm sure that my father had some colorful run-ins with some of the locals and that creature."

Realizing that her phone was our only communication with the rest of the world, she handed it to me.

"Thanks, I'm going to check that hole in the front before I call the patrol."

I walked quickly, almost running up the staircase before starting to dial the number. I didn't want to drop the phone anywhere except on the deck of the ship. I stared into the water, which was now black and foreboding and thought of our lost friends.

I walked to the interior of the boat and made my phone call. Of course there was no answer, so I left as detailed of a message as I could with my callback number. I sighed with disappointment and hung up the phone. I wanted to a take it down below, but something made me stare into the ocean for a moment. I felt the humid, sea air on my face and stared into the silence. All of the cruisers were back on the mega ship, and all of the lights along the pier for the shops and restaurants were dark. Every so often I would hear the rhythmic blowing of a distant freighter's foghorn and catch a flash from the main lands lighthouse, but other than that there was only darkness. I found it a little strange that the overhead lights along the pier were turned off. I would think that for safety's sake that they had to leave them on.

"This isn't the United States," I thought. *"They can do what ever they want. It sure makes it hard, however, to inspect the damage."*

The atmosphere and surroundings reminded me of being a young girl out here with my father. I can remember begging him to let me sleep outside under the stars and lasting about two hours until I had to go in because I was scared. I remember he and Mom arguing. It was the first time they had ever disagreed in front of me. Jonathan won the argument, but it didn't pay off because if they were looking for a prophecy, it didn't happen. Like I said, two hours later I was snuggled up between both on them. I also remember my mother warning me about the weirdoes on the pier after dark. I smiled to myself and wondered if I would qualify after our antics the other night. Even though they were arguing that night, I still remembered the togetherness that I thought we had ... us all being together in that bed peacefully. I remember the spark and fire in my Dad's eyes as he told the tale of the treasure to my mother that night for the first time. She could have cared less, but not Dad ... he was still thinking about it the next day. I remember that so well, because that was when he started searching for it.

It's strange what you remember. The next morning, bright and early, Jonathan was in the water and before Mom and I finished breakfast, he had retrieved some coins ... just for me. I remember because he laid them directly into my tiny hand with a big smile.

"These are for my special girl. Judy, you should save all of the gold coins down there."

I remember the disgusted look on my Mother's face when she turned away. I remember thinking, *"How could she do that? Here is the love of her life being happy and enthusiastic and she isn't happy for him?"* I guess that I grew up a lot that day. I went from not being able to sleep outside and crawling in bed with my parents like a baby, to noticing that they were never going to be happy or get along again. *"I think that I was probably 10 or 11 that year. It seems like so long ago and really it was, I guess that time flies by."*

I was deep into my memory bank when Jessica can out of the door. "Are you about done with my phone?"

"Actually, I didn't even use it yet. I've been just sitting here reminiscing about my parents and Chad. Did you find anything?"

Nodding her head she started to explain, "This is a strange place. Did you know a man by the name of Gregory?"

"Not that I can remember Jesse, why?"

"He was another friend of your father's. Gregory, Rollings and your Dad all knew about the treasure. The strange thing is that your Father was pissed off because Gregory got a new job down here with the harbor patrol. He and Rollings were afraid that Gregory would not share anything he found on his own and keep everything for himself."

I couldn't help but think that this was a really strange trio: an old fisherman, a Wall Street guy and his buddy, a Jamaican harbor patrol worker. It didn't make any sense.

"Did it say anything in the journals about my dad's friend, Michael?"

"Not that I saw, but I was just scanning. I want to get back on the internet and see about some of the other deaths around here."

"That's cool, and I need to call that harbor patrol guy. I left his card on the dining table."

"You kind of like that type …don't you?"

"You mean bald," I joked with her.

We started walking towards the door and I swore that I heard something moving in the water. Since it was so quiet, it grabbed my attention immediacy. I stopped dead in my tracks and asked Jessica if she heard anything. She answered no, but quickly stepped through the door, with me right on her heels.

It was a good thing that we went in when we did, because like always in the islands, a storm was directly on top of us. We could feel the boat shifting in the sea and I can only imagine being out on open waters and how rough the waters would be. As the captain, I wanted to keep Jessica as calm as possible, but I was afraid it's too late.

"What do we do now?" she asked, her big eyes frantically scanning the inside of the boat.

"Nothing," I answered calmly, "this is the safest place to be during a storm. We are warm, dry, and safe from that thing out there." At least that's how my father always explained it to me. However, it was really being a very rough storm. I could hear the wind outside blowing strongly and making the rain beat down on small, round glass above us.

"Man, it's really coming down out there."

I could hear the nervousness in her voice and rather than try reassuring her, I gave her another task. "You need something to take your mind off of the weather. Why don't we look up how many unsolved cases there are around here."

Jessica diligently tapped on her small phone and had the answer before the question was completely out. "27," she answered with gusto.

I was surprised by that number and just figured it was from the amount of tourists, or people unfamiliar with this area, or drinking too much and trying to ride a jet ski or parasail. I shared my thoughts with Jessica and she pressed a couple of buttons on her phone and was shaking her head no.

"That is just unexplained missing people, Sam. It doesn't add in the people that were here and reported documented incidents."

Well that blows my theory out of the water ...and speaking of water, I noticed a steady stream coming in or around the steel casing of the window. The storm was still raging outside as I concentrated on the leak. I assured myself that it would stop soon.

"I know that my father put that in for a couple of reasons. First, it was to let in outdoor light while down below and second it was to be an escape hatch if necessary. That's the one I never understood. I've never been down here when it rains this hard, maybe the leak is normal," I thought silently.

We continued rocking back and forth with the ocean waves and I kept one eye glued on the leak and noticed Jessica typing away on her phone.

"What are you looking up now?" I asked.

"Just seeing what type of sea monsters are around this area," she quipped.

I could tell that she found something interesting when she put her hand over her mouth and whispered, "I didn't know that."

"Jesse, you know that drives me crazy," I said loudly over the beating rain while sitting beside her. "What are you looking at now?"

"The Caribbean coral reefs are the most abundant with octopi, including the giant octopus. It is over 6 feet long from the top at the head to the bottom of the longest tentacle, and here is the part that surprised me. That same giant octopus can squeeze under a door!"

I looked at my friend with cross eyebrows and asked her, "Why are you even looking at stuff about those creepy things?"

"I guess because some of the missing person reports speculated that there might be one around here."

I laughed with my lips fluttering together like a horse, "You've got to be kidding!"

"Not at all!!!! Sometimes these intelligent creatures become territorial and protect other things besides their mate."

"You mean like maybe a treasure ... or a burial ground?" I asked.

Chapter 13

As the storm raged outside, even heavier now than before, I sat across the room from my friend listening about a strange, alien like creature, the octopus. Jessica was certainly giving me all the information I could stomach. Even when I was snorkeling with my father I didn't like those things, now the thought, I mean the reality of what I have witnessed and what happened to my two friends made those things catapult higher on my list. Maybe there was something to this air theory about territoriality. Then my mind and my eyes drifted back to the boat damage and leak ... then to the horrible death my friends must have experienced. Jessica kept describing the way that these creatures break open the hard shells of snails, clams, and other crustaceans with some sort of beak, while it draped its body over the prey. Like most things in the animal kingdom, it seems harsh and cruel, not to mention violent, bloody, and without any apologies. While she was teaching me everything I ever needed to know about the octopus, my eyes were drawn to my Dad's journals.

They seemed to start out mostly as a diary, you know, places that he had found to fish, bars and restaurants he had enjoyed and then it turned into a plan. A plan where he, Michael and Rollings were going to get rich by raising the treasure out of the ocean depths. He wrote about a native girl that he seemed to care for.

"That was fast," I thought. "His divorce wasn't final yet. It's always too bad to find out that your father was a son of a bitch, right under your nose."

I wondered silently to myself about this woman. I wondered what she had that my mother didn't and then why he would throw his family away for that. The lightning flashing caused me to look up from the journals. A bright flash of light caused me to look up and I swear I saw the large head and dangling arms of an octopus pressed against the leaky window. It actually caused me to lose my breath and I sucked in air immediately, causing Jessica to ask what was wrong. There really were a number of things wrong and I started feeling a cold chill come over my entire body. It wasn't just the chill of finding out that my "perfect father" was stepping out on my mother, or even the deaths of my two close friends. The chill went straight to the core of my body and for a moment I didn't know what it was. Then like being doused with a bucket of water, the feeling came clear. I was frightened, actually scared to death about being eaten or bitten by this, as my dad called it, "the devilfish." All of the sudden I felt lightheaded, almost like I was going to pass out. Again the lightning blazed away and I indeed saw the outline of a large octopus when I whipped my head around.

"That isn't really there," I tried telling myself. But I couldn't get that image out of my mind. I could feel my hands shaking and I knew all of the blood in my head rushed from my face and I felt like throwing up.

"Are you okay Samantha? You look as white as a ghost."

"I'm fine, but I don't know how you can read that, knowing that is how our friends died."

"I'm trying not to think about that."

"You need to think about it! We have not said goodbye to them properly, and that was our two friends in two days. How can you be that callus?"

Jessica looked offended and paused for a moment before answering.

"I'm not being callus... I'm trying to be practical. Do you really think I am that shallow of a person? It kills me that they are not here. My stomach hurts every minute since they have been gone. I'm trying to find that out everything I can about these things, so if we meet it, we know what to do. I'm surprised at you, normally you are the one figuring out a plan and I am the basket case."

She was right. Normally I am the one playing super woman, but I haven't been this time. Perhaps it's because somehow I felt responsible, being the captain and inviting. Or maybe I was dwelling on the breakup of my parents too much, either way I wasn't doing what my friend needed me to do ... and that stops now," giving myself a much needed mental pep talk.

"Can I use your phone," I asked?

"Yeah, sure, who are you calling?"

"I'm calling that patrolman Gregory. He is all over the place in my dad's Journal. Also he needs to know exactly what happened to our friends.

"But Sam, what about the hole and that leak? Aren't you going to tell him everything?

Are you ... I mean mentioning Rollings and everything?"

"I am ... we don't have anything to be afraid of. We didn't do anything!!! Let me ask you something. How old do you think Gregory is?"

"Probably our age ... why?"

"It's something in my Dad's Journal and just a feeling I got when we met him before."

"I don't follow you, Samantha."

"There is an entry where my dad talks about being in love with a native woman. Jonathan used to travel to this area frequently... right? Didn't Gregory seem to know a lot about the treasure?"

"He knew your boat, but other than that I and am not sure. I guess I wasn't really paying attention to him like you were, Sam"

"Put the pieces together Jesse," I argued. "Rollings and my Father wanted all the gold for themselves. Maybe Gregory felt that he should get some? Didn't you read me something earlier where my dad wrote that Gregory was going to work in the harbor? That would definitely give him more access to the gold?"

"Yeah I read that, but who says it's the same Gregory, or even the same gold?"

"Why don't we invite him over and ask him?"

She handed me her phone and I felt better than I had in quite some time. It's not like I had forgotten about my friends, or Rollings, or my Father. It was just a diversion for now and it was a hell of a lot better than dwelling on killer octopi. When I got her phone, I looked at the clock and it was after one in the morning. I didn't know that it was that late, but figured that maybe this would be the time to get service. Obviously I was wrong, because it went straight to voicemail. I really had more to say than I could leave in the message, so I just let it go.

"I'll call him first thing tomorrow."

"No answer," Jessica said looking through the journals. "I guess that it is kind of late. Does it feel like the boat is leaning, or is it just me?"

Honestly I hadn't noticed, but now that she mentioned it it does feel a little like we are tilted.

"It's probably just from the storm," I answered, trying to convince myself, but in my head I knew that it was from the crack I put in the hull. I decided to change the subject and gathered up all of the journals and we retired to the lounging area of the boat, just to talk.

"Let me put these things away for now Jessica. What are we going to do about Chad and Macy?"

Jessica and I sat and talked for a little while, discussing the fact that we didn't even have a body. Then we started our mourning together. I made us some drinks and snacks and after a good cry, we've shared stories about the two of them. I wasn't expecting to have our own private wake-funeral combination, but that's what it turned into. The storm continued outside the whole time we were talking. We covered a lot of ground, from my Father to my Mother and then back to our deceased friends. It had been a long time since we shared things with each other. We may live in the same city, but we really don't get together that often. Our conversation was just like it always had been ... honest, truthful, free and easy. The only thing that was keeping me from totally relaxing, was that crack in the boat. I could tell that it was making a difference in the way she sat in the water, but I figured that tomorrow when the sun came out I'd be able to examine it more closely. I wasn't worried so much about sinking as I was dreading the mess that I would have to clean up later.

"I think there you should be the one to tell Chad's parents."

"Why me, Sam? You're the captain and it happened on your watch."

"I don't even know them. You do. Besides what would I say?"

"Just tell them the truth. Hi, this is Samantha ... your son was killed by a giant octopus. I can't send you the body because this thing is keeping them for later. How's that?"

I could tell by the silly look on her face that she was kidding, but I had to think of something. I could also tell by that heaviness of our eyelids, that we were battling the need for sleep, which could explain her silliness.

"Come on Jesse, I'm being serious."

"Does this island have some sort of newspaper? If it did we could it just e-mail the story to them."

She giggled out loud which I didn't really understand. Perhaps she was drunk or just incredibly tired, either way it was still a terribly impersonal idea. I noticed the tilt of the boat becoming more pronounced and I told myself that I can't wait for sunrise, I've got to do something now.

"Shit, too late," I lamented as the power to the boat went off.

Jessica began freaking out. "What's happening?" she questioned. "Are we going to die? I don't want to die, Samantha. You've got to do something!"

I did the best I could to settle her down, talking the way friends do to each other.

"You're not going to die, just because the power went out." Apparently the combination of booze and lack of sleep had hampered her ability to think clearly.

"Why don't we just go to bed," I suggested. "It will be light in the morning, which is only a couple hours from now. Once the sun is up, I will be able to of check out our situation."

"Do you think that we will be safe in here?"

"Safer here than we would be sleeping on the deck," I promised.

"What if that thing tries to get in?"

Sounding like a mother, I calmed her down with a joke. "I told you not to watch that scary movie before going to bed."

"I can't help it, I just keep thinking about all of the things the octopi can do. They are supposed to be very intelligent, crafty, and we know this one is territorial. And all of those coins, maybe he sees them."

"Now you are talking crazy Jesse; how would an octopus survive out of the water?"

"I don't know, maybe he fills that balloon -like head with water so he can survive. I don't know, but if this creature can lay on the bottom of the ocean, with all that pressure, and still survive, he will find a way."

"Take a moment to listen to yourself. It's just an octopus, nothing more. Now let's try to get some rest."

I heard her mumble something under her breath and asked what it was. I had to ask a couple of times before she answered reluctantly. "I said OK it's just an octopus that is 6 feet long and has just killed two of our friends! Don't be scared? Good night."

"The last thing that I wanted to do was argue with my only remaining friend from this trip. She was absolutely correct, this thing had killed our two friends, and who knows if it may be possible to live on land by filling its head with water. I guess that I will find out tomorrow."

Chapter 14

I felt a cold, an almost wet touch on my shin. I didn't pay too much attention, because by now I had been asleep for at least a couple of hours. Jessica's rhythmic breathing and even a little snoring forced me to move from my chair to the other bed, which was full of used towels that hadn't been throw in the dryer. My plan was to hang them out on the back, but things were crazy today. I cuddled my pillow like a stuffed animal; all of in a dream world of my own. I felt the wet on my shin again, which was fine until I felt it high up on my thigh. At the time I was dreaming about my Father. I missed him and longed for the days that we used to have together on this boat. I shook my legs spastically trying to get rid of the sudden sanction of my leg being wrapped around. I woke up enough to see that everything was still dark around me. As I thrashed around in the bed, my dreams turned from my Father to a much more sinister creature. *"It was the devil fish!"*

I felt the arms starting to corral me, just like it had done to Chad. No matter how hard I pushed or pulled, I could not break free. I tried breathing, but my mouth was full of salt water. *"Now what," I thought in a panicked state as I was pulled under again.*

I heard the lightning and thunder crash and I saw the vison of this hideous creature on the window just as I earlier today.

It was the same ghostly white color as my boat and it had two large eyes. The eyes did not look completely through you. It's just like they were there, black and lifeless. It looked like this beast was straight from hell. It had no eyelids or face that I could determine. I felt its grip getting tighter, and I imagined what Chad felt like during his battle. In my dream, I gouge at its eyes, but they just disappeared. It was almost like I heard taunting laughter coming from the beast while its grip slowly, but surely continued constricting my upper leg. During the struggle, I tried using my other leg to break free. However, that didn't work and now both of my legs were trapped. I tried crying out, but again I received a throat full of salt water. Things were getting desperate and desperate times call for desperate measures. With both of my hands I pulled my thigh near my face. It took nearly every bit of energy that I had left. *"How did Chad jet the hell out and of this powerful grip"* I wondered as I wiggled around. The creature turned from white to an angry red, almost glowing. I thought that my only chance to get free might be by biting my attacker. As gross as it was, I put one of the thick arms into my mouth and a bit down as hard as I could. Once again, I heard the laughter. It was a deep belly laugh echoing throughout the room. I could not get my mouth completely around the large leg and I wondered if this <u>thing</u> imagined that I was some sort of small mosquito or other pest just trying to irritate him. I thought that was why he was laughing.

"How did he get in here to begin with? Was Jessica okay? And where is she anyhow?"

I reasoned that he must have come in under the door. It was just like the show we had been watching. That's when my struggle when to the next level. I didn't want the same fate that happened to my friends or my Father. I was going to do what ever I needed to to avoid that crushing parrot-like beak which loomed near the middle of this strangely adapt creature. While being pulled in the same direction by multiple arms I opened my eyes; something you should never do under salt water. They stung and burned immediately, but again the creature just laughed.

"This is really some way to go," I lamented, *"On my own boat, tied to the dock."*

I wasn't about to give up completely. I scratched and poked and bit everything that I could to try to free myself, but it seemed as if things got worse. I could tell that I was being sucked into the center of the creature, because everything around me it was black. I remembered the horror of those major films and I felt like one of the sea snails.

"When it totally engulfs you; you can't get it out and it's over."

I fought even more ferociously than I had before, cursing and twisting, trying to move away and then I felt a large hand on my shoulder. "Its okay … wake up, Sam."

Immediately, with a sudden start, I jerked awake to see not only my friend Jessica smiling, but the harbor patrolman as well. Both of them were staring at me and smirking. At first I didn't understand why, but the more awake I got the more I started to realize my surroundings. There I lay, covered in towels, with one even in my mouth. I was so embarrassed and said the only thing that I could have. "I guess I was dreaming," I declared rubbing my eyes.

"You were really struggling with something that's for sure," the Jamaican pointed out.

"What where you dreaming about," Jessica asked?

I checked discreetly to see how I was dressed before sitting straight up in bed.

"I wonder what they would say if I told them the truth? I wonder how long they had been watching. I guess that it is a good thing that I was only dreaming about an octopus and not something more sexual. I am already embarrassed enough."

"I guess that I was having a nightmare about everything that has gone on during this trip."

"Yeah, your friend was telling me."

"I wasn't going to say anything about the coins, but he noticed these strange ones lying around, so I told him everything."

I raised my eyebrows when I looked at Jessica. "Everything?" I asked.

"Yeah, I mean why not, he's a friend of your Father's, so I figured what would it hurt."

"What's wrong with her?" I asked silently. "Wasn't she paying attention to what my Father had been writing? This guy was all my Dad talked about towards the end so I need to find out what they knows about this treasure."

"Miss Samantha, your Father was a good friend of mine. We went fishing together and drank plenty of rum. We even discovered a lost treasure together. He was a good man. He and Rollings both were good men."

I was starting to shake off the cobwebs and wanted to hear more about my Father.

"What was the plan for the treasure, Gregory?"

"Plan … there was no plan, at least as far as I knew. Did Jonathan say there was a plan?

I didn't really get a chance to talk with him before he passed away, I mean. I remember that he always wrote things down in his journals. Have you been through them?"

"He certainly seemed to know my Dad, but I was curious to what extent. I didn't really have time and it's not my style to beat around the bush, so I tried to go about it as politely as I could"

"How do you really know my Father?"

"I came to know Jonathan through my job and other things around here like the villagers and their acquaintances."

I had heard just about enough of this bullshit, so I came straight out and asked him.

"Are you my half brother? I know from these journals that my father was fooling around with an island woman. Was she your mother?"

The long pause answered my question for me, but I still needed to hear it. Gregory stumbled over the answer, but his large, white smile said everything clearly even before he spoke. "I was sworn to secrecy. Jonathan was a wonderful man so I figured that we would meet one day. He provided money not only to my mother, but me as well. He wanted me to grow up healthy. It can sometimes be a struggle here on Conger. He told me all but you, what you are like and you sound a lot like him."

I appreciated compliment, but was it really one? "Is that why you were so lenient with me when I first reported my friend was missing?" Was it because you knew you were my half brother?"

"You might think that, but it isn't true."

He placed his sunglasses on top of his head, nervously shifting them from his shirt pocket. I could see a slight tremble in his hands, as he did this. His voice cracked when he explained the real reason why.

"No, that's not the reason ma'am. It's something else."

I had to drag it of the nervous young man by asking, "Well what then?"

"It's the devilfish!!!"

Jessica looked up from reading the journals immediately. I can tell that she was as interested as I was, so I asked Gregory exactly what he meant. "Jonathan, Rollings, and I found that treasure after we bought an old map one day when the fish weren't biting. We did it as more of a joke than anything. There are a lot of legends or superstitions around this place. You know, old fishermen have a big catch one day and are always looking to repeat it, so they turn to witchcraft, lucky charms and everything else. There have always been rumors around the village that the treasure is guarded by an octopus. For years I heard this story and I never believed it. And then I got this job and was on the inside. I knew what happened everywhere around this pier. I knew when the drunks where coming out of the restaurants and bars and I got to know the owners and I also heard many stories about the octopus and the treasure. At first it was no big deal. I mean with the coral reef around here, we see thousands of them, so I wasn't worried. That is until I saw this one. Its arms are reach over 6 feet long and it is always seemed to hang around this pier."

Jessica jumped in to the conversation, "Okay, so it's big, but I have been doing some research and I have never heard of a man eating one. I can't find any evidence that one has ever been recorded."

"That's because they have never examined the bodies at the right time," Gregory explained. "These creatures are masters of fitting in to their environment and surroundings. There have been many unexplained deaths around here. The same lead always states that it is people disturbing or trying to take the gold. That's why the majority of it is still down there."

"I've never heard of such a thing, Gregory."

"Samantha, what happened to your Father, Rollings, and your friends?"

I didn't really have an answer or good explanation, or even a piss poor one for that matter, but Jessica did and she answered for me. "Do you see those coins over there? They were in the possession of our friends at the time they were killed. I can't explain it, Sam can't, but what ever is going on around here is wrong! There may be more truth to that rumor than you would like to admit. Our one friend Chad was taken right off of the boat. He was wrestling with it earlier in the day, but only after he stole some coins. As for Rollings and Jonathan, the report showed that Jonathan was killed, not dead from a heart attack, like Samantha always thought. Tell him, Sam ... tell him what else we saw."

Rather than launch into my story about the young man I saw taken from his boat, I looked closer at Gregory. He has some of the same mannerisms as my father and some of the same facial expressions. It was especially evident in with his eyes and the way he tilted his head when he was listening. I really didn't know what Jesse wanted me to tell him and I was still wrestling with the fact that I had a brother to begin with. Thankfully, it's not part of me to feel sorry for myself and I'm one of those girls that just pass on forward, no matter what, but what I have discovered is that being 30 year old sucks! Since I have turned my third decade on this planet, I've lost two of my best friends, found out that I have a brother from an affair my father had almost 30 years ago and that my Father didn't die of a heart attack. And now I am being asked to believe that a large sea monster is after us, all because of some coins! It's too early in the day for this. Both Jessica and Gregory were staring at me to make some sort of comment.

"Hell, I didn't know what to say. But damn it, I'm going to say something."

I took a deep breath to relax myself and then started in. "Gregory, you seem like a nice man, but do you really believe all this devilfish bullshit?"

"I believe that something killed your Father and your friends. But do I believe in a sea monster? Not really!!"

"Just so we are on the same page. Would you like some coffee?"

"Yes ma'am, thank you. I haven't been on this boat for years, I have always been curious about you."

I smiled shyly as Jessica brought us some coffee.

"I suppose that I would've been curious about you also, if I had known that you existed. My father wrote about your mother in his journals, but I didn't know." And as soon as that statement left my lips, I realize that it didn't matter. I didn't care that this was my half brother; I didn't even care that Jonathan stepped out on my Mother. And honestly five years ago it would have killed me, but I have learned that people are people and they will make mistakes, just like I did with Macy. That was a defining moment in my life realizing that everyone is made up of good and bad and what defines you is how you react to this decisions that you have made. At that moment, the sun seemed a little brighter, the water a little clearer and my mood went to a whole other place. It was the first time that I didn't feel that pressure to be the perfect Samantha. I could just be me, which is a very special person in itself.

It seems as if Gregory and Jessica noticed some sort of visible change, I could see it in their eyes.

"What else does the legend say, Gregory," I asked?

"Well, it says that whoever disrupts the treasure will be cursed and tracked down by the devilfish."

"But what about those other people," Jessica asked? "They were not going after the prize yet they were still killed."

"Over the years this creature has found that it enjoys his humans. I know, I know, it's really strange, but it would really clear up some cases and get them off my desk."

"You mean that you have unexplained dead people out there, Gregory?"

"Unfortunately yes, but we have no bodies ... not a one. The legend says that these victims will be taken to an underwater grave and stored there until the curse is released."

Jessica and I looked at each other. It was obvious that this guy believed the legend. Sure, it's a little far-fetched, but everything is really is different down here. However, I still had to interrupt his story.

"You mean that you as a law man will let people go missing, without any supporting evidence and just blame it on some legend?"

"This is a remote island, Samantha and we are trying to do the best we can."

It's a remote island, yes, but that's not why you are keeping this quiet, I thought to myself. It's because of the tourists.

Jessica was rudely doing something on her phone, maybe checking into the legend or something. I hit her thigh with the back of my hand to make her stop and that's when she looked over my shoulder and saw it. "Oh damn," she exclaimed with her hand over her mouth and talking very softly. I turned to look and immediately had the same expression. Gregory had in his back completely turned away, but from what I could tell it was a dead body floating towards our boat.

"What is it girls?" Gregory asked with his usual accent and smile before turning and dropping his sunglasses overboard due to his shock. "Sweet mother of Jesus!"

We rushed to the front of the boat to get a better look. I really wish that I wouldn't have done that. A severely disfigured upper body was floating towards us, face down. It appeared as if many sea creatures had been feasting on the bloated cadaver. There were nibbles taken out of each arm and one of the legs had been eaten completely off. There was no blood thankfully, just saturated skin and hair. Jessica and Gregory were both fascinated and horrified by the find and rapidly went for the hook too lean out into the water and corral the body. I wasn't nearly as interested in seeing the body as I was interested in the water starting to come into the boat. I guess when the three of us moved suddenly to the front it submerged part of the boat and it started filling in on the area with water.

"Hey guys, um… there is water getting in."

But neither of them seemed to care, they were absorbed with this body which kept drifting closer and closer to us.

"Of course it will get closer to us," I thought silently still very worried about the water getting in. "The more you pull at it - the closer it will get to you and the more water will rush in.

"I almost have it Gregory."

"Bring it over here Jesse, it seems like I can get a better angle from here."

While the two jockeyed for position on the boat and continued poking at the body, I couldn't watch any longer. I thought they were being disrespectful, pulling and poking at this human body like a piece of discarded trash or a dead fish. They were having trouble containing any enthusiasm. It disgusted me and I felt the need to tell them so.

"You guys don't need to sound so excited about finding a dead body."

"We are not excited. We just need a little help over here," Jessica struggled to get out.

They were relentless, using oars and the hook as more of a team now with much better success. It wasn't more than a few moments and they had the body (what was left of it) flipped right side up on the deck.

"Oh, damn!" Jessica yelled dropping the oar into the water quickly.

"What is it?" I wondered aloud.

"It looks like a female Caucasian to me."

I snuck a glance and it was a female Caucasian … it was Macy. She was still half dressed, probably from her struggle, and not only bruised but disfigured. I forced myself to look again and was almost sick. Seagulls flocked over and around the body trying to pick at it. I can't imagine what Macy or her family would think about how her body was being treated. Jessica forced Gregory to give her the hook to shoo away the birds.

"Get away you dirty birds," she yelled swinging the long handled hook. The birds moved away and unfortunately I saw my friend in the most horrible state imaginable.

I didn't want to look, but like a car accident, I had to. She had several large holes around her skull, almost like she was hit with a hatchet. The birds or some other sea creature had eaten one of her eyes. That was all I needed to see and my coffee was overboard. Gregory brought me a towel while Jessica leaned over her friend's body screaming and crying.

"I'm so sorry Gregory. I just... I don't know... I just didn't expect it to be that disgusting."

"No problem, I'm sorry for you. Were you guys friends a long time?"

"Yeah, almost as long as I can remember," I answered.

My heart was still racing and I felt a tad light headed, so I stayed seated. It was amazing but Jessica was still spending time gently examining her best friend's body.

"Hey Gregory, come over here for a minute."

He snapped to her quickly and excused himself from me politely. I couldn't hear everything that they were saying, but I did get the high points. Jessica was questioning Gregory about some of the injuries and what might have made them. I don't know how she did it, she was closer to Macy than I was and normally she was the one that would get sick. Maybe somewhere inside I felt just a little bit responsible. My Dad always told me that anyone who boards the boat is my responsibility. I wondered what they were going to do with the body and that's when I heard them talking.

"We can do the ecological thing and feed all of these animals," Gregory suggested.

"I think that's what Macy would have wanted."

"Bullshit," I thought, "she would never want her body to be used as fish bait, bird food, and shark food, or even as food for the devil fish, if it does exist.

"I don't believe you Jesse. Don't think that her parents would want her body to have the burial of their choice. You know that they would."

"She was very environmentally active though."

"Doesn't it bother you at all that you have to talk about Macy in the past tense?"

"Of course it bothers me, Samantha, but what am I supposed to do now?"

"There is a policeman on board, let's ask him."

For the first time this morning Jessica agreed with me and asked Gregory was else we could do. He hesitated for a moment for some reason and then offered assistance.

"I suppose that I could take her to the morgue."

No kidding, why that hesitation? I was through messing around, getting sick of seeing my friend mistreated. I wanted some answers.

"Gregory, I know that we just met and you are my brother."

"Half brother," he answered.

"Okay what ever, but whenever my Father knew that his answer was not going to be popular, he would pause just like you did. What are you afraid of?"

"It will be more of a hassle, and to find out nothing."

He was afraid ... afraid of putting that body on his boat for feat of the curse.

"You're afraid because of that legend aren't you?" I asked.

"No, I'm not afraid; I just want to respect your friend, that's all."

I wasn't going to let this drop and pressed for a straight answer.

"Don't you think it would be valuable Jessica, to know where those hatchet looking marks came from?"

She was still examining the body when she answered, "I'm sure that her parents would like to know and I've seen marks like this before. Haven't you Sam?"

To be honest, I hadn't really looked that closely, but I was inclined to blindly believe my friend. She is still propping up Macy's head and presenting it towards me, so I felt I had to look. It was gross and disgusting and I felt very bad for Macy, but when I looked the wounds were familiar. "They look just like Rollings! I'll bet that they are identical and even in the same location."

"You're right Sam that is what I was thinking exactly. Gregory, what type of ocean animal makes the marks like this?"

He kind of avoided eye contact, while shifting his weight back and fourth.

"It might be hard for you to understand it, but legend is sacred around here."

There was something about the way he said it that made Jessica and I think that there's a lot more to this.

"You have seen these markings, haven't you?" I asked.

"I don't know how to say this …. but yes, on our Father."

I didn't know how to react, I stood there with my mouth agape not believing Gregory at first, but then I did and was overwrought with motion. In some way Jonathan would have worn his ocean death like a badge of honor. He would have thought that it was a very noble way to go; doing something he loved. But I looked at it a completely different way. I pictured him struggling for air, trying to reach the surface and being dragged down by this <u>thing</u>. What he thought was noble, was awful for me to recount. It brought the lives of Macy, Chad and everyone else who has fallen victim to this <u>thing</u> more into focus. I knew that Gregory is the local authority and I have no right to ask this of him, but I am still going to.

"Let's go to the police station," I commanded. "We need this body to have an autopsy complete immediately."

Gregory waved his hands and proclaimed, "Once I tell the examiner where I found the body, she won't touch it."

"So don't tell her … right Samantha?"

I nodded in agreement with my friend and we used some beach towels and a large trash bag to transport the remains. I felt a little bit guilty when the three of us were carrying her body from my boat to Gregory's.

"Thanks for taking us. It doesn't look like mine would have made it."

"Would you like me to tow it in," he offered.

I looked at <u>The Sammy</u>, which was beginning to tilt towards the front right and happily boarded the patrol boat. "It would take too long to transfer all of our gear and supplies. The electricity is still working, so it should be fine, but thank you."

I looked back at the handicapped vessel and wondered what I would tell my Mother. As I looked back, I saw some ripples in the water and they eventually formed a brief whirlpool. I tried to get Jessica to look but it was gone already. With the harbor patrol, we slowly made our away towards the station.

"The whirlpool is following us, I believe; or is that from our propeller, or just my imagination?"

Chapter 15

I kept looking behind us as we cruised the short distance to the station. However, I couldn't tell if something was following us or not. Jessica noticed and asked me, "What are you looking for?" I didn't respond because we were at the station. I helped Gregory tie up at the pier and Jesse helped him with the bag containing Macy's remains. When I actually thought about everything, it was so very, very sad. She only came down here to celebrate with me. I know she brought along her annoying boyfriend, but right now that didn't seem nearly as big a deal as it was a couple days ago. The police station was as I expected it to be. It was very cramped, dirty and smelled strange. Thankfully the sun was shining brightly overhead, because without it, I'm sure that it would be dark inside. I say that because the building is made from a very dark wood. In fact, everything was the same color and I noticed only one computer strategically placed in a common area. I was still having trouble getting past the smell. All I could think of was that it smelled dirty, like wet socks. Jessica and Gregory came in with the bag and went directly to the back office. Someone must have heard them and a round faced, black woman with long hair tucked up underneath her white cap came out of the back room.

"Gregory, is that you?"

"Yeah, it's me mom and I have a couple of friends with me and some work for you."

That is the woman my Dad cheated with, I wondered silently.

"Come around here man, you better not be bringing me too much work," she threatened in a perfect Jamaican accent.

"Okay, I can buy that he was attracted to a native woman, but I never thought that my Mom would be replaced for an older version."

"What do you have in the bag son and who are these two lovely young women?"

Jessica and I stood stiffly and silently with our backs to the wall and then she whispered, quietly to me "That is the woman your Dad was sleeping with?"

I didn't have any explanation except for, "I guess so."

While we stood there feeling embarrassed and like intruders, Gregory swiftly walked by us over to his mom to kiss her cheek.

"I see what you have been up to," she smiled, "and who are these girls?"

"They are friends of mine and this, this one here is my sister."

The woman lit up like a Christmas tree, smiling from ear to ear. "Oh, let me look at you. You are so beautiful, isn't she Gregory?"

It was like he knew this was going to happen. He apologized quickly to Jessica but then quickly turned back to me. "Don't you just love her long, black hair?"

I really didn't know how to react, so I just stood there, like a dork, smiling. The woman could not take her eyes off me. She just stood there smiling and repeating, "I can't believe it."

"Well, you'd better because there she is," Gregory insisted.

"And look at the beautiful suntan you have."

"The reason we are here mom is because one of their friends got killed. Something smells good, are you making lunch?"

"Yes, but I don't have enough for all of us."

If lunch was the stench hanging in the air, I'm not hungry.

"I am so sorry about your friend, what happened to her?"

Jessica stepped forward in front of me and politely asked, "We were hoping that you could tell us. I would also like to say

110

what a nice young man Gregory is. You should be very proud of your son."

The pair looked at each other and started snickering. Jessica and I felt like we were on the outside looking in. We looked at one another and shrugged our shoulders, but they just kept on laughing.

"You are very kind - both of you, but I'm afraid I'm not his mother, I am his mother's older sister."

"Yeah, and she does mean older, by like 10 years," Gregory claimed.

"I just was going by what you said. I mean you called her mom."

"Yes I did Samantha, but I have called her that since my mother died."

Jessica and I felt terrible now; I mean what do you ask after that? I decided to not say anything and let him share the story if he wanted to.

Gregory and his aunt didn't offer any details but instead started to dish out whatever it was that was filling the room with that horrible odor. They politely offered some to us and Jessica accepted. I guess this area was more like a lunchroom, but they made us feel so at ease, that it felt like they had invited us into their home.

I'm not really sure what they were eating, but it didn't look or smell appetizing at all. I'm not sure if Jessica was just being polite or not, by trying it, but I wasn't about to. I thought that it was cute, every one holding hands and praying before the meal. And a police station, with this backdrop of a sun scorched sky and dusty surroundings would have made a fabulous picture. I may have declined the food, but I said yes to the lemonade. I didn't know when it would be the right time to bring up our friend, and what happened, so I just let them eat and continue their conversation. It took until the second plate for Gregory and Jessica to start bringing up some details.

"You see I call her mom, because ever since my mum passed away, Tillie has watched over me," Gregory told us.

"That's right. Some folks say that I have a son with out getting to enjoy making one," she laughed.

"I know some women back in New York would say you also lucked out by missing the labor," Jessica smiled politely.

"I don't know about all of that, but I hope that you girls are not doing what Gregory's mom was doing."

"Here it comes," I dreaded silently finishing my lemonade and bracing for a sad tale.

"How did she pass on?" I prodded.

That's when I got the surprise of my life. Without hesitation or reservation, Gregory jumped in and shouted, "She was attacked by the devilfish!"

"Gregory, you shouldn't spread rumors. I told you a hundred times that there was no such thing."

"What type of thing is he talking about," Jessica asked.

"Can you believe it … a full-grown man at 40 years of age and he still believes in a local legend that has haunted this island since I was a little girl. If you listen to the legend, there is some sunken treasure in the harbor being guarded by a gigantic octopus. It's the silliest thing."

"It's true and you know it. That's why I was waiting until after lunch to share the body that I brought. It has the same markings and injuries as my birth mother did."

As they cleaned off their plates of the remaining scraps from lunch, they continued to argue about Gregory's mom.

"Do you really believe in a giant octopus," Tillie questioned.

Back and forth they went. Gregory firm in his beliefs and Tillie not backing down from her nephew. I wanted to remain objective, but I had to pick a side.

"I-I've seen it, "I added standing up from the table like kids used to do in class.

Tillie shook her head and rolled her eyes while saying, "I'm not surprised, since you are his sister. I would have bet money that you would back him up."

"It has nothing to do with him," I promised. "It has to do with my two lost friends."

"And it has to do with her Father, and his friend, and all the other suspicious deaths going on around here. This place is supposed to be a tropical paradise and instead it is a feeding ground for a monster. She is right mom and if we don't do anything, we will be setting the table for this beast. You have refused to examine any of the other bodies that I have brought you, which I believe are other victims. I know that you are upset about how my mother died, but perhaps if you had examined her body, we'd know what we are dealing with and if we need to bring some one else in here in."

"Yeah," I agreed, "there has to be someone out there who is curious enough to want to find this thing."

Gregory looked at his aunt and it was obvious that they were both hiding something. Even Jessica, who is not normally focused in, picked up on it. For the first time since Macy and Chad were gone, I saw fire raging in her blue eyes.

"There's more to it ... isn't there?" They both looked directly down at the wooden floor but didn't answer.

"You are both supposed to be public servants. What is it that you aren't telling us? My Dad has a lot of money and I am used to getting what I want, so you better just tell me. I have lost two friends and you lost your mother and father mysteriously and you're not saying anything? What the hell is going on," Jesse demanded.

This is a waste of our time, let's go Jesse."

I was ready to forget about everything and just go to the Coast Guard and I told them so, but Jessica talked me out of it by bringing up a possibility. "I'll bet that the cruise lines pay a daily sum of money to use this pier, so maybe some of that money has been funneled to you guys."

"Yeah, I could see how that happens Jesse, and I bet your father with his connections could get to the bottom of it pretty quickly."

"How much is it really worth to you Gregory to finally have a clear conscience?"

"I bet it not nearly as much as the cruise line is paying them to doctor up their reports, even though they know it's a lie. That's why you went out on your way to tell me the medical examiner will not look at a body with those marks. You didn't want us to know that this has been going on for years. My father, our father is dead and you don't give a damn! All you care about is lining your pockets, both of you! Well I have had it, we are calling the Coast Guard and putting an end to this bullshit charade. Come on Jesse, let's go!"

We stormed towards the door and were going to leave, but Gregory stopped us.

"Please, don't go, don't report us," Gregory begged, "I'll tell you the whole thing, and so will she. You called us public servants, that's exactly who we were trying to serve, the public. We knew that if we came out with a story about a man -eating octopus watching over a lost treasure, no one would believe it. But both of us had seen it, many times."

"It's true but we weren't breaking any laws. We just keep our mouths shut."

"She's right and when the money started coming in we just didn't ask or tell."

"Gregory is telling the truth. We were getting paid but actually the same thing has gone on for years."

I took up the questioning now. "How long has this legend been around and killing people? Why didn't you ask for help?"

"That's when the money started to come in every week," Tillie admitted shamefully. "I stopped looking at the disfigured bodies when my sister was killed. I knew that it wasn't the right thing, but I thought maybe the octopus would die or go away. I never thought that it would live this long or cause so much trouble. I'm sorry."

Her apology didn't carry much weight with me. All I could think about was my Dad and two friends, not counting the others that I didn't know personally, who were victims. The more I've thought about it the more pissed off I got.

"Are you really that stupid," I asked myself about Tillie. You never thought that this legend was coming true right in front of your eyes. You're the medical examiner for Christ's sake, you should be a little more on the ball."

I guess that I didn't hide my frustration very well because both Gregory and Jessica read my feelings easily.

"We knew that taking the money was wrong, but I felt like someone owed me something after what happened to my mother."

"Being mad is not going to bring back our friends, Sam."

"No, I realize that, but maybe they wouldn't be gone if somebody would have said something sooner," I fired back in an angry tone.

"I know that it's hard for you, Samantha, but it's hard for me also. I lost both my mother and father to this thing. I want this monster dead and away from my island. I have had enough of the legend and even more of the truth!"

"But Gregory, you don't even know if these deaths were caused by the same thing." Jessica interjected.

"My aunt could tell you for certain. She could tell all of us, couldn't you Tillie?"

"Yes sir, but for the record I don't believe in the legend. An octopus killing folks, come on."

"Please say you will do it," I begged.

"After my sister died and I heard the rumors, I stopped examining claims about this legend. I didn't believe it then and I don't now, but let's go into the back and see what you have.

Chapter 16

I couldn't believe my feelings of elation about having my friend Macy's body examined. I guess when I thought about it ... it was morbid in a sense, but we needed to know what happened. Jessica was trying to download the information she could on her cell phone about the octopus. Jesse is a fast learner and retains facts quickly. Actually, she can be a little annoying while we are playing a game of trivial pursuit, with her knowledge of most subjects. I thought that the outer office was bad, but when we got into the back room, it was even worse. I know that this area is for cadavers and they really wouldn't care, but I'm not sure how long it's been since this place was cleaned. There were cobwebs in all the corners and on the vents. The lighting for the entire room was a circular, glass fixture that hung directly over the examining table. It was dark as could be around the areas surrounding the table.

As we walked into the back at Tillie's insistence, I felt a little lightheaded.

"Maybe you are hungry," I thought to myself. It was a good thing that my stomach was empty, because once the examiner put on her mask and gloves, she wasted no time it freaking Jessica and I out.

Gregory suited up as well. He held the tape recording device as his aunt started describing what she was looking at.

"The victim appears to be a healthy, female of approximately 30 years of age. Examining the arms, I notice small bites all over, probably from being in the water and having small predators take a bite as they swam by. Not at all unusual and what would be expected for someone that has been in the water for 24 hours."

It amazed Jessica and I how matter-of-factly she picked up and handled each part that Gregory gave her. She examined each one under the bright light briefly, turning it over and examining at it from all angles. The skin on her arm was sunburned looking and shriveled, like you had been in the water too long.

"One of her legs has been completely severed near the pelvis. It appears not to have been a clean bite, due to the victim's struggling and thrashing about."

"She is talking like Macy isn't even a real person …. just a plastic doll with missing parts"

I thought about what her final moments might have been like and then I thought about my Father. What was it like for him? Did he struggle and fight back? My mind switched to the visual image I had of Chad wrestling for his life with this awful monster. I remembered the angry red glow of its skin during the struggle and wondered if that was the only time the creature looked like that. I thought back to the scene of this <u>thing</u> under the Caribbean water, gliding along like some sort of alien. I thought back to its large eyes looking both vicious and lifeless at the same time. What other tricks did this creature have up his sleeve? It changes colors, squirts ink, can taste and grip with its oversized suction cups on each of its eight legs. It can lay on the bottom of the ocean because it has no bones, and it can also fit under the door, or other confined spaces if it needs to. Now it is killing my friends and family. I really didn't need to remind myself of that, but I did need a break from listening to Tillie. Jessica could tell that I was not listening in and she startled me by clapping her hands loudly.

"Here comes the most interesting part, Sam. Tillie is now beginning the examination of her head. Look at how disfigured it is. It is like it not even her, it's more like a mannequin."

I couldn't help but say it aloud, "But it is her. Look at the look on her face," I insisted.

I guess that Jessica was in her full crime scene and investigative mode and was watching every move they both made. It was all I could do to keep from throwing up the more she manipulated her head, and kept narrating.

"There are cuts and contusions throughout the skull. Gregory, you said there were birds flocking around the body, the do you think they might have done this?"

"Perhaps the eyes, but they're not strong enough to get through a human skull."

"The bite pattern represents one of a very aggressive creature …one that is not only defending its territory, but with a purpose to kill."

Jessica could no longer sit silent and blurted, "How do you know that its intent was to kill?"

Tillie turned the head around and pointed to a particularly large incision on top and near the back of the skull. "You see … this victim was actually trying to get away and this thing kept on coming, like the devil." She stopped herself and actually had to put Macy's head down on the table.

"What is the matter mom?" Gregory asked his aunt.

However, she could not answer him. She started crying and turned away from Macy.

"I can't do it anymore," she wailed.

"Why, what's wrong?"

She did not give Gregory a straight answer, instead just continued to cry. I guess that she got all of her grief out for now as she stopped the examination momentarily to settle down. I didn't want to be in this examining room in the first place but since I was I felt the need to help her to a chair. With me on one side and Gregory steadying her on the other, we managed to sit her down. Jessica brought Tillie a glass of water, which she gulped down quickly.

"Thank you dear."

"Are you okay now mom?"

"Yes Gregory, I'm okay now."

She may have said that, but I could see that she was still shaking.

"All these years," she mumbled, "and I didn't believe. Gregory, it just became obvious to me that what killed your mother and a lot of the other people has surfaced again recently. I never thought that it was possible, but it is. Gregory, I have never said this before but you need to **kill that beast!!** All these years, all these bodies, including my sister and I've been lying. ... as well as lying down for the money. You're not any better Gregory," she warned wagging her finger at her nephew.

Gregory looked around, shrugging his shoulders as if to say, "What else should I have done?" "What was I to do? You didn't believe the legend, even after I brought you the up victims. Hell, it even killed your sister, and you know it."

"Don't you dare talk to me that way ... I've done everything for you," Tillie fired back.

Jessica and I felt that we were in the middle of a family dispute, so I changed the subject ... well, sort of. "So professionally you are saying that the devil killed our friend?"

If nothing else, my comment lightened our somber mood somewhat. I saw a smile creep onto Gregory's face.

"No my dear, I am just clearing my conscience a little. It makes me feel a little better to know that I hadn't been stealing that money all these years."

"Are you saying now that you believe the legend?" I asked, thinking about my Father.

She clapped her hands together and answered, "What else could it be? The body went through a significant horrific struggle. I have never heard of a man eating octopus, but maybe this one is different."

"Are you sure that is what causes those marks," I asked?

"Yes, they are very distinctive. The places on the skull and the depths of the incisions leave no doubt in my mind. I remember five or six years ago when I saw this particular pattern, I knew that there would be an expert available on one of the cruise lines. She taught me specifically what to look for and claimed that this <u>thing</u> is probably about 6 feet in length. I didn't want to believe it, but then I heard the legend from Gregory and it all made sense."

I was kind of half listening, but mostly I was thinking about my Father.

"That's what killed your Dad, you do know that, Samantha."

"That's exactly what Rollings told me. He even showed me the certificate of death. Did you sign off on that Tillie?"

"I will look through my notes if you want."

Jessica, who had been very quiet and looking for something on her phone, finally spoke up. "No need to look through your notes. I found it on the internet. You mentioned that the cause of death was undetermined up here, but down here you checked the box that says you would attach an explanation."

"The cruise line would not let me. I wasn't the only one. Gregory did you fill out a truthful form?"

I could see that he was becoming agitated at not only the questions, but the insinuation.

"I don't want to talk about that right now. Mom, you now believe right? And this girl, she was killed the same way?"

His aunt answered with a nod of her head and Gregory continued to be pissed off.

"If there is nothing else, I'll take you girls back to your boat."

"What happened to the hospitality, the friendliness that this island advertises? It seemed to all go out the window when Gregory got the confirmation from his aunt. It was time to leave and leave now."

Chapter 17

G regory started out towards my boat, but I noticed a little more determination and speed than when we came to the station. It was obvious that the autopsy had impacted each of us. Just the thought of bagging up her remains is still weighing heavily on my mind. It was like it wasn't real. I almost expected Macy to be smiling, holding a drink and waving from my boat. I knew in my heart that wasn't going to be the case, but my mind still pictured it. Gregory had the motor wound up so there was no conversation. The more I thought about it, it is possible that he did this on purpose so we didn't have to rehash what we were all feeling. I still wanted some questions answered, mostly of Gregory and his aunt. Like how much money had they each collected over the years? Or how many bodies and other young and old people had suffered the same fate as Macy or Chad, or my Father? As we jetted through the harbor, leaving a wake behind us, I wanted to scream to each and every cruiser frolicking in the warm waters that there was danger below, but I didn't. I don't think that they would've heard me, or even cared as I looked at the smiles on their faces.

I thought back to my state of mind and remembered that we wouldn't have listened or cared less until something happened. I'm sure my Father felt the same way and I'm pretty positive these people would too. Does that mean I shouldn't even try? Shouldn't I have given my best effort? Maybe if Jessica and Gregory join me in shouting the message to everyone, it would work.

"You look troubled my sister," Gregory shouted towards me while backing off on the motor.

"It's been a very interesting and terrifying last couple of days. Hell, I didn't even know that you existed before yesterday. I lost two of my best friends and witnessed other attacks by this monster along with finding out the truth about my Father. Then I had to put up with watching my friend get stuff in a trash bag and examined. It hasn't been easy to say the least!!"

"I …. it's been nice meeting you and your friend Samantha, I just don't know how to a express my apologies. I saw the sadness on your face and surprise in your eyes when you found out about my aunt. I should have really told you before we got there."

"You should have told me any number of things."

"I guess so, but I'm new at this big brother thing."

I sent him an apologetic look while Jessica, who can't stand to be out of the loop, walked to the back of the boat to join us.

"I see that you finally put down that phone."

"I was taking pictures of that giant cruise ship that we passed. Man, those things are big and my battery died," Jessica frowned. "I didn't plug it in last night because there was no power, but I figured it would last at least until we got back."

"I am surprised that it lasted that long, I mean you were on it all morning."

"I was accessing records, learning about octopi, and reading the legend of Conger."

"Did you find out anything different," I asked?

"Yeah, a lot of stuff. Do you know Gregory, that there have been over 20 unexplained deaths since you and your aunt started getting paid?"

That quickly got Gregory's attention and he turned the engine down to a crawl, so he could hear well. I didn't mind because we were almost back to my boat.

"How many," Gregory asked, "are you sure?"

"There have been 23 to be exact," Jessica stated with certainty and continued. "The legend started as a rumor between two best-selling concrete companies, one of which lost the contract and was trying to stick it to the other guy in hopes that no one would sign up to rent the pier, but it didn't work. The dock was rented immediately and that company has been paying you ever since to keep quiet."

"But there is something out there," Gregory answered, "and what about the coins? I know that they are real."

"The legend goes on to say that the loser in the concrete war actually rose, in captivity, in a special cage of concrete. The concrete box was made of a porous material that allowed water in, but the creature could not get out and it was a giant octopus with an appetite for human flesh. It killed its handler and got free in the early 1990s and now is roaming free. These are very intelligent and adept creatures, they must have been feeding it around here and the divers poking around the treasure are a great supply of food, that's why it still lives here."

Gregory appeared shocked, but then sounded somehow vindicated. "See, there was truth behind the legend all along, just not the truth that all these old fishermen believe in, it actually has some factual basis. My next question is how do we kill it?" Gregory did not want to hear the solution as he smiled while putting his sunglasses down over his eyes and asking again, "But again …. how do we kill it?"

I can tell that Jesse wasn't comfortable giving the answer, but she did. "The only way is to spear it through the heart with a knife, but you can't get that close to it because of its long arms. Many have tried, but no one has done it yet."

Gregory smiled that same confident smile as he had earlier holding up his harpoon and saying loudly, "I bet they didn't have one of these."

I didn't say it out loud, but I was pretty positive that it was just his machismo coming out. *"There's no way that he stood a chance fighting hand to hand with that monster; we needed a much better plan."*

I was trying to come up with one on my own, listening to Jessica and Gregory discuss the tendencies of this particular octopus and then I saw it. My father's pride and joy near the horizon listing badly towards the hole in the front.

"God damn it," I shrieked pointing at the boat and shouting, "Look at my boat! I knew that some water was getting in but not like that."

Without hesitation Gregory picked up the pace and we were next to the boat in no time.

"Wasn't it leaning that badly when we left?"

"Hell no Gregory, if it had been, I don't think I would have left."

"I wonder if our stuff is okay."

As we moved in closer, I started seeing garments and towels floating near the boat, which told me that the inside was also flooded. *"It wasn't that big of a crack to do this much damage."*

We moved in and I couldn't wait to climb aboard. This boat was my Father's estate. I couldn't imagine his face right now. Some clothing, some loose papers floated near the <u>Sammy</u>. It looked like hell, all junky and broken down looking. Each time I looked it was like a knife stabbing me in the kidneys. Some of the best years and most influential times of my life with my Father, my Mother were here on this boat. There were so many special times and things I learned to do. My Dad showed me how to tie different knots, how to use the GPS, how to use a reference point on the land to help guide me ... it certainly was some of my most cherished memories. When we came down here, it really seem like we were getting away from everyday hustle and bustle. Until recently, like the other day, I wasn't aware of any unrest or arguing between my parents. This is just our retreat, a place for us to be a family and a place where my Father could safely, without interruption, imagine a fantasy or two about being a pirate. To me all those good memories and optimism for the future were sinking along with the boat right now. I felt a small tear beginning to form in the corner of my left eye, so I wiped it away to avoid a full on gusher. Jessica came over and apologized for the first time since she had startled me.

She squeezed my shoulder gently and said, "I'm sorry Sam, I didn't mean to startle you and I sure as hell didn't mean for all this to happen."

"Yeah, I think you'll need me to tow you in this time."

"Well Gregory you are the expert and the police, what do we do next?"

"I will fill out the proper forms, but first let's see how bad it really is."

Gently and somewhat acrobatically we helped each other to get from Gregory's harbor patrol boat to the Sammy. It really was kind of freaky, because it was so silent on board. I was used to laughter, jokes, and old stories being told and retold in the main living room. There was at least a foot of water everywhere on the main deck. There was no cruise ship in port so the pier was not its packed, lively self either. Jessica walked through the ankle deep water to the main state room.

"I'm going to see how much of my stuff is still there."

"I'll go with you Jesse, just to see how bad it might be."

"You guys go ahead, I'm going to try your radio again and maybe get someone out here, Gregory yelled to us as we were walking away.

We sloshed around and of course the interior was a complete disaster. Some of our clothing was floating and of course the inflatable recliner used for catching sun rays was about to drift into the hallway when I opened the door.

"This is ruined in here," Jessica announced. "I'm sorry Samantha, but this is awful."

I could hear Gregory trying over and over to reach some one, anyone on the radio, but without any luck. I wasn't worried as much as I should have been about the financial loss this would cause my Mother. I looked out of the sliding glass door, which was now angled severely to the right and I saw the same thing again near the pier.

"*There's that whirlpool again,*" *I thought frantically. "This time I'm going to tell someone.*"

"Hey Jesse, look over there," I commanded forcing her to look away from her ruined clothing. After a few questions about where I was pointing at, she finally saw it just in time.

"You mean that circle that looks like water going down the drain. What do you think it is?"

"I'm not positive, but every time I have seen that on this trip, someone has wound up dead. I believe it's the devil fish!"

"Do you think it is surfacing to get a better look?"

"I didn't know that. You have become the octopus expert."

"Okay, I watched a couple of films and now I'm an expert. You should know me better than that Samantha. Wasn't it you that said I needed someone to make my toast for me?"

"I never said that. That's bullshit! Who told you that?"

"Well, I heard it somewhere ... just the other day," Jessica argued.

"This is dumb! Let's just gather all the important things we can and go back to Gregory."

It wasn't but a second after I said his name that I realized I could not hear him trying the radio anymore. *"Oh God," I thought, "every other time I've seen that whirlpool, someone has ended up dead."*

Jessica noticed the worried look on my face and asked me about it. I told her that not only had I seen these ripples in the water before but I also saw what made them and it was pretty scary. My heart started pounding has my adrenaline kicked in. This <u>thing</u>, whatever it is, killed my Father, my two friends, and the others as well as now destroying this boat. I'm not going to let it take my brother without a fight. I listened closely for Gregory's voice, but nothing. That made me even more panic stricken.

"What if I'm not able to send out a distress signal? And then I remembered we are just off of the docks, we could swim if we had to. Oh, um ... what was I thinking? Neither of us is going in to the water with the devilfish out there."

That was when I realized that I needed to calm down and analyze the situation. It's not like me to act frazzled in stressful situations, but that's exactly what I was doing. I took a few deep breaths and scripted a plan.

"Jessica," I shouted, even though I didn't really need to. "Do you still have the rope that we threw to Gregory?"

"Yeah, but it is soaking wet. What do you want it for and where is Gregory by the way?" she shouted back in the same high-pitched tone.

"I want you to tie one end around your waist and give me the other end."

She did as I requested even though she wasn't sure why. Jessica continued picking up some clothing items out of the water, which is now becoming substantially higher inside the boat. What was originally just covering the tops of our feet was now up to my shin. I couldn't tell any more even where the leak was located due to the height of the water. Perhaps there were multiple holes for all I know. I wondered silently where Gregory was and after tying myself to Jessica, I thought we needed to start looking for him on the upper deck.

I explained that the rope was to keep us from getting separated. It probably was not one of the best ideas, but at least I would know where she is. The rope is at least 25 foot long, so there is a lot of slack between us and we could move about freely. The securing of passengers together was something that my Father would do with me, when he might fall asleep fishing and watching me. That's why it didn't seem as weird to me as it did in Jessica. The standing water made it difficult to walk, but only slightly … just like wading through a shallow creek.

"The last place I saw Gregory was over here," I commented pointing towards the radio area.

"I don't see him," she answered, looking around.

Gregory wasn't anywhere to be seen. I thought about some of the facts that Jessica had shared earlier about those strange octopi, especially how they moved about while hunting so then I started watching where I stepped. It would be just my luck that that thing was around here. Then I saw another one of those whirlpools starting just near the front of the boat.

I quickly tugged on the rope to get Jessica's attention. "You see that?" I asked her.

She nodded her head and added, "I have seen those too."

"Where is Gregory? Is it possible that we are too late," I thought to myself while keeping one eye on that whirlpool.

I thought that if there was going to be any activity, it would happen around the swirling, clear water. I squinted and tried to shield my eyes from me evening Sun. With Jessica still tied to me, I felt a severe pulling action from her and I thought maybe she had spotted something. So I quickly crossed the midsection of the boat and when I got beside her, I couldn't believe what I saw. Without warning and completely to my surprise, in the center of the whirlpool, some thing was surfacing. I half covered my mouth and sucked in air when I saw what surfaced.

"Samantha ... look!!!!" Jessica shrieked.

Chapter 18

A t first it was difficult to see because of the sun glare, but finally I could make out the figure ... it was Gregory! He was coming up from the bottom and holding up the harpoon that was from his patrol craft. I was not embarrassed to share that he had scared the hell out of me.

"What are you trying to do, kill us?"

That is when I saw it for the first time. The expression on his face, with one eye closed and wiping his mouth, he resembled Jonathan. Obviously Gregory is somewhat darker skinned than dad and has a totally different hairstyle, but I have seen my father had that exact same look on his face thousands of times. What was making it hard to see, was the bright reflection coming off the silver plated spear. He pushed his diving mask up on top of his head and excitedly yelled, "You guys need to see this. There are hundreds of those gold coins under your boat. They are all ours for the taking, come on in."

It seemed to me like Gregory was forgetting the danger in this ocean and possibly a little gold struck at the sight of all the coins. He wasn't concerned about my boat anymore, or anything. All he could talk about was the amount of coins on the sandbar below. I can understand why Jessica didn't seem to care as much because she's already a rich lady, but I at least expected her to show some concern about our sinking vessel. She didn't and much to my surprise she undid the rope that was holding us together.

"What are you doing, Jesse?"

"I'm having fun ... maybe you should try it some time."

"What??? How can she even think of fun? We are sinking, have lost two friends, and there is a monster in the water. I guess that's why, I don't know, we never got any closer in our friendship. There are just times when she becomes a total "blonde" and forgets the situation."

I whipped my head around in a huff and senselessly went to the radio to give it one last try. I could still hear Gregory and Jessica talking wildly to one another in between trips down to the sandbar. They were giggling and laughing like a couple of teenagers diving in the community pool. I heard them challenge each other to see who could gather more. I really didn't want to be the wet blanket and spoil their fun, but somebody had to be responsible.

I yelled to Jessica, as she stood on the sandbar with the water just covering her breasts.

"Where is your phone?"

"It's in my other pants, but it doesn't have any charge left."

Mumbling to myself, "Maybe there will be just enough for me to send out an SOS."

As I walked back to the bedroom actually I waded knee deep as the water continued rising. I was looking out of the windows, but not really paying attention, until I heard the scream. It was one of sheer terror. It was high pitched, but I really couldn't tell who it was. I forgot about what I was looking for and turned around quickly to find Gregory and Jessica both screaming loudly.

Once I got outside, it was easy to see why she was freaking out. "Get it away," she yelled pushing the water away from her.

Upon closer inspection I realized it was Chad's body floating towards her. His body had been somehow torn in half at the waist. I wondered to myself if possibly a passing boat had done that, or was that same horrible creature of the sea. This scene was worse than it was with Macy, if that could be possible. I tried to look away from the body which was bloated from being in the water for hours and obviously Jessica was trying to do the same thing but it wasn't working for either of us. In exactly 3 seconds after seeing the body, she was by my side on the deck of our sinking boat. We hugged and I promised that everything would be okay, but honestly I knew our lives would never be the same after this trip to the ocean.

We were shaking and crying. I was keeping it together better than she was, but I wasn't in the water seeing the body floating up to me. I searched everywhere for a dry towel, or something to wrap her in but everything on the floor was soaking wet and then I had a thought. *"The bedspread, that should do it."*

I waded to the guest bedroom, ironically where Chad and Macy had slept and grabbed the comforter. It was ironic because I could still see Chad's body floating when I looked out of the sliding glass door. It's disgusting and I have no idea how Gregory could be so insensitive and oblivious and that his only focus was on recovering the gold. He continued diving down and surfacing with more gold coins. He looked like a little kid retrieving change that his mother had thrown in to the pool.

"I am going to say something to him about being disrespectful," I thought.

And then I remembered what I was doing. I rushed the blanket to Jessica and she wrapped herself up completely in the blanket.

"You'll be okay, just try and catch your breath and relax."

My words fell upon deaf ears as Jessica continued to breathe quickly, with her teeth chattering un-controllability as she scanned the harbor. I had no idea what she was looking for and to be honest, I was still completely freaked out about seeing Chad. She pointed in the direction of Gregory and tried communicating something. I went over and held her, squeezing her tightly to try and make her settle down, but it wasn't working, She just pushed me away and as I looked out into the water ....that's when I saw it!!!!

Chapter 19

I couldn't believe what I was seeing. It was like something out of a science fiction movie. It was an octopus but MUCH MORE!!!! It was the biggest creature that I had ever seen and it was breaching the water like a whale. Almost as if this thing wanted me to see its face. I looked and it was a horrible and terrifying sight its large balloon- like head, which is colored scarlet ... a mad scarlet, from its head to the tip of its long eight arms. Each one of them looked to be as big around as my own leg. That head was unique, compared to any octopus I had ever seen. The reason was the large black eyes. It almost looked like an alien invader. While its color gave me the impression that it was angry, its eyes did not - they remained black and lifeless. I shouted to Gregory out of instinct and fear. "Watch out! He is after the gold!"

I don't know if he heard me over the slashing of this beast. It was very strange, because unlike a tiger or a lion, this creature did not make a sound. It took Gregory a few moments to focus on what was happening. He stood on the sandbar looking in the direction of the splashing and obviously didn't see anything because he did not run towards the boat. He stood tall with the water coming up to his waist. The creature was definitely close by and I yelled even louder trying again to warn him.

"Gregory, it's still out there! Drop the gold, damn it!"

"I've got the gold. Don't worry," he answered obviously not hearing me correctly.

"Jessica, Jessica I could really use some help over here."

I could tell by her reaction that she heard me, but she did not answer, not with words anyhow. Like a mute she pointed towards the back of the boat and made a noise, a low growling noise to get my attention. I looked back quickly to see Gregory trying to climb aboard. He actually had a smile on his face as he was climbing the steps. He was near the top rung when a thick, scarlet arm grabbed him around the neck and yanked him back in the water. The strength and quickness surprised me. The creature was spewing an ink- like substance everywhere… in the water and on the back of the boat. I rushed to the back, because Jessica was being no help whatsoever. She just stood there frozen with fear. Gregory, in the mean time, was screaming and doing his best to fight the creature.

At one point during the battle, he reached down with his harpoon and dropped it on the deck. That was when I reached for his empty hand. I had it!

"Hang on Gregory. I have you," I shouted.

He tried answering, but the thing pulled him under and he got a mouthful of salt water and ink. He was thrashing around with his other arm while still trying to hold on to my grip. I don't know if it was that, or the sheer strength of the creature, but I could feel my grip slipping.

"Jesse, come and help me," I grunted, but there was no response.

I feared that she was gone; I mean she just stood like a statue wrapped up in a blanket watching us struggle and appeared to be in a total state of shock.

I reached for the long harpoon with my other arm while still trying to hold on to my brother but my strength appeared to be no match for our predator.

"Don't let go," I pleaded with him.

I grabbed the long, slender, silver harpoon with my other arm and swung wildly at the beast. I think that I hit it squarely, but I'm not sure if I did any good or if I made it worse. I could feel the resistance increasing and out of desperation I screamed,

"Let go of my brother you slimy son of a bitch!"

But the creature did not let go, as a matter of fact it won the tug of war with me. Try as I might, I couldn't keep my grip with Gregory on the stairs and he was pulled completely under the water again.

I tried stabbing the head, but it didn't work. I obviously didn't penetrate his skin since I don't even think it was bleeding. I saw through the clear, Caribbean water that Gregory was pulled completely to the side of this octopus and its long arms totally wrapped around my newly found half-brother. I could see Gregory continuing to struggle, but I knew that it was just a matter of time now.

"No!" Jessica screamed loudly coming out of her catatonic state. Then she continued talking quickly with her New York accent, "Do you know what happens under there? That thing will eat through his skull. That's what it did to all of the others. That thing has a beak and it is so solid and hard that it cuts through anything. It cracks open snails, clams, what ever it wants."

This was too strange and I couldn't believe it was happening AGAIN!!! Minutes ago she wouldn't say a word, and now she is talking nonstop, throwing out fact after fact. It really was disgusting thinking about what was happening to my half-brother under the webbing of the devilfish. I watched the struggle out of the corner of my right eye until I couldn't watch anymore. I watched until the water turned from clear to blood red and then I couldn't watch anymore. I knew the devilfish had once again claimed another human close to me.

As I stood on my slowly sinking boat I thought back to before we arrived. This was supposed to be a celebration and instead it has turned into a horror movie. All I wanted to do was get out of here. But how? This creature, legend or not, seems to have taken a particular interest in me, my friends and family. Did I believe it was actually plausible that this creature knew that we are stealing from it? The scientists and biologists all seem to believe that the octopus is one of the smartest creatures on the planet, but can it really remember? Can it really have a vendetta against a certain family?

Jessica was still mumbling quietly to herself, so I went over to her and grabbed her by the shoulders. Shaking her awake from her trance, I saw her large blue eyes open widely and I knew that she was back. "Are you okay now?" I asked.

She unexpectedly lurched towards me and wrapped her arms around me. "I'm... I'm so scared I don't know what to do. What are we going to do? We are going to leave aren't we? Please tell me we are."

"We are going to leave, but on our terms and after killing this thing," I announced confidently.

I trudged through the standing water, which was now up to my knees on the Sammy. My parent's main investment was in the process of going all the way down and I really didn't want to think about that, but I had to. My family and the security of his getaway to Conger was always the driving force behind Jonathan's long hours on Wall Street. After meeting Gregory, I have to reevaluate things. I have two look back and give my mother a break. I mean he was cheating on her for Christ's sake! No matter what those journals say, he was no choirboy. I almost forgot what I was doing and realized if we were going to get out of this alive, I needed to do one thing at a time. First, kill the devilfish and then worry about all this other bullshit.

"Jessica, do you see anything out there?"

"Not really, it's getting dark in a hurry."

She was right. It was almost like the sun dipped into the sea in 10 seconds, from the last time I noticed. I was not going to let the darkness, the death of my half-brother and my friends deter me. I was going down fighting, just like Gregory and my Father did but hopefully I won't go down at all.

Chapter 20

Not only was it getting dark quickly, there was also a fine mist and fog settling in. I could feel my thick, black hair wanting to be released from my ponytail holder due to all the dampness setting in, but I didn't do it. The mist was clinging to my body everywhere, but unlike NYC it wasn't all that cold. I had a plan, but to execute it, I needed Jessica. I was trying to go for my Father's diving knife but the case had floated away.

"Damn it!"

"What are you looking for, Samantha?"

"I was looking for something sharp to stab that <u>thing</u> with and I don't know where my diving equipment is." With the fog settling in and getting thicker, I heard the eerie sounds of a fog horn in the distance. For some reason that sound has always reminded me of a lonely woman calling out for her man.

"I didn't find the case you were looking for, but something sharp just jabbed me in the back of the knee."

"Grab it if you can; it's probably that harpoon from Gregory's boat."

Jessica reached down almost up to her elbow in the water, on the back of my boat. She pulled her hand away quickly. "Something just went by me."

"Are you sure it wasn't the harpoon floating by?"

I could tell by the look on her face that the answer was going to be no.

"No, it was a slimy and just darned away. It was like a fish or something."

And then she stopped and stood very still, looking everywhere. "Do you think it was that, that devilfish creature?"

"Did you find the harpoon?" I asked.

"Yes, it's right here by my foot. Your boat is sinking fast, Sam."

I didn't need her to tell me that. I looked and found some things that we could make a raft out of since there were all sorts of things on a boat that will float. From coolers, to the refrigerator, to the actual life raft, but honestly, I wasn't all hyped up to be in the water with that <u>thing</u> after what it just did to Gregory. I was trying to put it out of my mind, but how can you? It closed around him so fast and pulled a strong swimmer under the water without any problem whatsoever.

"Samantha, are we going to be okay?"

It took me a moment to put on my game face to try and make her feel better, but I knew that I was going to lie.

"Hell yes, as long as you have that harpoon. It will be better than a knife anyhow because we won't have to get as close to it to kill it."

I was standing with my legs apart mainly for balance and that's when I felt it swim by. It felt a little like Jell-O as it brushed the inside of my thigh. I couldn't really see anything except for a shadow, so I couldn't accurately judge how large it was, but I felt it on each of my legs, so I knew that it was at least one to three feet across. The darkness and fog took over the entire pier and for the first time I felt the nervousness and anxiety that Jessica had. I thought back to the bodies and remains that we had came across and realized that even though I didn't really know my half brother, there was some sense of security having a man around.

"That's bullshit Sam and you know it. You have gotten where you are today without men being around constantly and this is no different."

Jessica was obviously having this same feeling of loneliness as I was. I heard her walk through the water towards me and towards the lights on the pier. I got a glimpse of her worried eyes. "That <u>thing</u> is on here with us, isn't it?"

I didn't want her to completely lose it, but I was pretty sure that giant octopus was around here somewhere.

"I felt it earlier, but I don't anymore."

"What are we going to do Sam? This <u>thing</u> kills people. It doesn't discriminate, or care, it just kills people! What are we going to do? We have no means of communication, our boat is disabled. What are we going to do?"

I don't know why it took me so long to think of this, maybe I was trying to block his death out of my mind, but we still had Gregory's boat. I'm sure that it has working electricity, a radio, and fuel to get us to the station. I managed a wry smile with my discovery and actually was pretty proud for my calm thinking in an emergency situation.

"We have a boat, Jessica."

The confused look on her face told me everything. I'm sure that she was so focused on the terror we had witnessed that she completely forgot just as I had.

"We have Gregory's boat," I exclaimed, "It has everything we need: power, radio communication, everything. If this <u>thing</u> wants this boat and everything on it, he can have it. What he cannot have is us!"

"Great thinking, Samantha. That's why you are the captain and not me."

It wasn't like I didn't hear her, but my focus was drawn to somewhere else on the boat. I heard a slight sound of movement in the water and that grabbed my attention. Jessica obviously did not hear it, because she continued talking.

"I was pretty scared at first, but you have made me feel a lot better. I always knew that you were the smartest of our group."

I appreciated her compliments, but my attention was still drawn to that area of movement on the boat. My eyes were now fully adjusted to the darkness and the fog was another story. Jonathan used to tell me that the fog plays tricks with sounds. He said that you might hear something off the starboard side, but it's really in front of you, or behind you. I started to think that maybe I was tricked when I heard something swimming around, but then I heard it again and it was right around my feet! I wanted to say something to Jessica about it, but rather than frighten her even more, I just allowed her to keep talking away.

I looked down quickly hoping to catch a glimpse of the creature, but if it was hiding from me and doing a great job of it. Then I remembered the coins laying in the galley and the main living area as well as the master bedroom.

"I wonder if that is what he is after?" I thought silently. "Maybe that's why he went after Gregory, because he was diving for those coins. If that is the case, as the legend would have us believe, we should be fine just leaving the boat.

"Jesse, you did some checking up on the legend, right?"

"Yeah, before my phone went dead."

"Does the legend say that this thing is guarding the gold," I asked?

"Yeah, but that's not the entire story. You remember when I said that octopi are highly intelligent? There were studies that showed some of these creatures are more involved than others and they can remember certain things. They studied it by injecting them with a dye and then running MRIs on their brains. The brain would light up when they came in contact with any familiar smell, taste, or even visual recognition"

That was starting to sound a little far fetched to me and I was just about to explain that to her when she let out a blood curdling scream.

"It's got me!" she punctuated with a blood curdling scream.

I looked down and snaking in between her feet and climbing towards her ankle I saw it. It was the very beginning of a long arm. It was blending in with the water and the white top of the boats deck.

If it hadn't been for the suction cups I don't know if I would have spotted it, but there it was. Somehow it began climbing up Jessica's left leg. The thing that was weird to me was that it did not climb like a vine on a tree, but it was sticking out on its own … just out there, almost levitating until grabbing her leg. Still holding the harpoon I had taken from Jessica earlier I jabbed at the creature's arm.

"Watch my leg," Jessica warned.

I was trying to be as precise as I could, but this devilfish could pull her under at any second and she would be gone. I looked away from where it was wrapped around her and there was another spot further out on the deck that I could see another of its arms. I rushed through the standing water and stuck the harpoon deep into the thick, transparent looking arm with all my strength. I winced when I drove the sharp end in, almost as if I was doing it to a person, or as if it was making some sort of noise … but it wasn't. The deadly arm released its grasp almost immediately.

"Let her go you bastard," I shouted as I pierced one of its arm. "The gold is on this boat and you can have it!"

Jessica moved towards me and gave me a hug. "Thank you, thank you, I thought that I was done for."

"If so you kept it together very well," I complemented. "No crying or anything."

"I didn't want you to miss and get me so that's why I was so quiet."

Just then, I heard some movement in the water again and looked around feverishly. It was no use, I couldn't see anything. It was like everything was even darker. No wonder…. that's when I noticed that some of the light poles had flickered out.

"Enough of this," I said with no regard for the sea monster. "We need to get from here to Gregory's boat as quickly as we can."

Jessica nodded in agreement, but I really don't think she knew that we were going to have to jump from one boat to the other.

"I'll grab my phone and put it in my pocket so we can charge it when we get there."

I made it seem like that was a good idea, but Gregory had a radio on his boat. So I really didn't think that the cell phone was that important, but I know how people are about their phones, so I quietly agreed.

"Grab that and anything else you want because this boat is going down."

She scurried quickly past me splashing through the water towards the back of the boat. I stood silently in the foggy, damp air, hoping to hear something and then praying that I didn't. I couldn't hear anything special, except for a passing freighter. The fog horn, I could tell, was getting further away. I had my harpoon and was holding it like some sort of gladiator, guarding what was left of my territory. I walked to the back of the boat, with my spear in hand for defense. I noticed another one of the lights flickering and about to go out. It was the one directly over the rear of the boat, providing the most light for us.

"Jesse," I yelled, "let's go!"

I clapped my hands together and it echoed off the surrounding mountains, but did nothing to hurry her along. *"I guess that I have to go back there," I lamented under my breath heading into the most flooded part.*

The Sammy now had a distinctive lean to it, and I knew that it wouldn't be long till is was totally submerged. In my mind, silently, I said my thank yous and goodbyes, for all the memories. This was the one place where Jonathan could truly be his own man. It was here away from the gray granite of Wall Street, the constant ringing of the phones, and apparently the nonstop bitching of my mother where he could just be himself. I allowed myself a moment of reflection, and could tell that time was growing short.

"Jessica, can you hear me," I shouted fearing that she had been grabbed once again.

I felt a tug violently around my waist and before I knew it I was sprawled on the deck. I don't remember what I yelled, or if it was just a noise, but I yelled something and Jessica came running. I struggled mightily to break free, but it was no use. The creature had me and was pulling me towards the edge of the boat. The surprise attack not only caught me off guard, but made me drop the harpoon. I lifted my head not only to stop swallowing salt water, but to turn and see this beast. It looked exactly like I expected. It was the angry red color, that strange balloon-like head and those lifeless, black eyes; with eight, large arms flailing away in opposite directions. I don't know exactly how large this creature is, but it certainly had strength to spare. It was pulling me, without much effort towards the side and I was wiggling and squirming and shouting the whole time.

"Oh my God," Jessica loudly exclaimed when she finally came out from the back.

"Do you see the spear?" I struggled to ask.

She did and was reaching for it immediately. The waves were now on the inside of the boat and sloshing back and forth, because of my struggle with the beast. That made it a little harder for her to grab the long handled harpoon as it floated on the deck. She would reach in one direction and then we would move in the other. After what seemed like hours, but it was only mere moments, she grabbed the spear.

"I've got it," she exclaimed!

"Good, now start stabbing," I instructed.

"Where, at your waist?"

By now my hair and clothes were soaked and I continued to try and break free by pounding the beast in the head, which gave me an idea.

"Stab him in the head," I directed.

She moved a little closer and took a half swing towards the thing. I figured that it would just be a glancing blow because of her animal loving nature. It was even worse than that because she dropped the harpoon.

"Whoops," she exclaimed and then she was struck by one of the other arms and knocked to the floor of the boat with me.

"Now what?, I thought.

Chapter 21

T he battle continued with us both scrambling to reach the long, aluminum weapon. We each had a hand on it from time to time but couldn't grasp it and I could feel the devilfish's grip starting to get even tighter around my midsection.

"Finally we both have hold of it ... now let's jab the sucker," I instructed.

Based on her previous performance, I knew I needed a better grip on the shaft. I reached my arm towards the end of the harpoon for more leverage. "Okay, now on three," I shouted aiming directly for one of those large eyes. I counted down and after each the number we were able to swing back and forth in unison until we got to the number three. The stab was perfectly placed into the devilfish's left eye. Immediately I felt its grip loosen and I drove it further into its head. The creature slinked off the side of the boat falling into the clear water of the harbor. Elated, we met in a joyful embrace at the center of the boat.

"I think that you killed it, Sam."

"You mean we don't you?"

"I'll take a little bit of credit, but you were the one that was pushing the harpoon into his head with much more force than I was able to muster up. When did you get so strong?"

Rather than stand around chit chatting, I thought that now would be the time to get on Gregory's boat. I didn't feel totally confident that we had killed the monster and was concerned that he might rise again out of the water.

"Let's get to a boat that is not sinking before we really celebrate."

We moved to the front of my boat, which was now taking on water profusely. The front of my boat was actually getting so low in the water that we were going to have to take a downhill jump to get on Gregory's boat. I helped Jessica along since she was having trouble slipping on the tilted, soaking deck. I was under impressed with her strength, I don't know why, because she's always been a pampered Princess most of her life.

"Hold on to the railing, it will help you keep your balance," I advised.

"Okay, but I don't know if I will be able to jump. Sometimes I'm not very coordinated."

"In her world of butlers, chefs, and maids, I'm sure she would rather have one of them make the jump for her, but today she had to do it on her own."

"It's really not all that far. You can do it Jessica." The distance between the two boats was maybe 3 feet, but the trick will be landing safely.

"Hurry up, before <u>The Sammy</u> is almost completely under water," I prodded, because I had to jump after she was successfully on Gregory's boat. Begging and encouragement were not working so I had to try another tactic. "We need to get off now ... God damn it" I shouted. "Do you want to be in the water with that <u>thing</u>?" She shook her head no.

"Then jump or we will be!" I saw her tentatively let go with one hand and she started towards the deck of Gregory's boat.

"That's it," I whispered to myself, knowing that in about a minute we would be completely under.

Jessica took the leap and let go with her other hand. It was like I was watching her in slow motion. The jump was not very far, but she had psyched herself out so much that when she made it, it was like she had won a gold medal. She raised her arms in triumph and shouted, "That was great!"

I nodded in agreement, but she had taken so long that the water was almost up to my waist. I let go and saw my Dad's pride and joy continue to sink to the bottom of the harbor along with his journals, and rum and of course all the gold coins. I observed a moment of silence for the boat named after me and then I started to worry again about that devilfish. I'm glad that I didn't need to swim very far, because the harbor water smelled awful. I guess it was the gas and diesel fuel brought in by the boats, lying on top of the water. I was pulling myself out of the water when Jessica leaned over to assist.

"This is great, let me pull you up."

I really didn't need her assistance, but she leaned over anyhow, head just above the water.

"That's okay Jesse, I have it." I'm not sure if I actually had it, or if I was just letting her off the hook, because I saw how weak she was. It didn't matter, she insisted and grabbed my elbow which was near the top of the ladder. Like lightening and out of nowhere, a large something pulled her into the water. It had to be the devilfish. Jessica was pulled from the boat and now was in the water with this thing.

"Jesse," I shrieked while pulling myself onto the boat.

"Sam," she yelled back with panic in her voice.

From my new vantage point on the deck, I felt that I would be able to see more, but it was still very dark and foggy. I knew that this boat had underwater lighting as well as a spotlight somewhere, I just didn't know where.

"Swim to the boat as fast as you can and don't look back, Jesse!" I was amazed at how far she was knocked off of the deck. I kept telling her to swim while I fooled with every button I could find. None of them were working until I found the one by the ignition switch and the underwater lights came on.

The first thing I noticed was a whirlpool beginning just behind Jessica and then I saw it. It is the biggest, most ferocious looking octopus I had ever seen, on television or in person, swimming right at her heels. She was kicking and stroking as hard as she could, but she was no match. The octopus was on her in a flash. He pulled her away from the boat sending her towards the middle of the harbor. I tried not watching, but I had to. This <u>thing</u> is so quick that I didn't even have time to shut off the underwater lights. He pulled her into him and started to drape his entire body around her.

"Oh no!!!" I gasped. "I know what happens next."

Jessica didn't even get out a scream. She tried fighting and I could tell that by the amount of bubbles in the water. However, the battle did not last very long. She didn't have any type of weapon with her, so I wasn't surprised. I was in survival mode and started searching for my own weapons. Unfortunately, right now there wasn't time for remorse about Jessica, or any of my friends.

Now I was scared to death!! And I should be this monster has killed at least 10 people that I know of and I am sure its sights for set directly at me. I knew that I should immediately radio for help, but that's not what I did. I scoured Gregory's boat for something, anything sharp, to be used as a weapon. This creature had taken all the people in the world that I love except for my Mother away from me, so I wasn't going anywhere until I destroyed with son of a bitch. I turned my head away from the bloody water to look for a knife, or another harpoon. I didn't find anything in the immediate area surrounding the driver's console, so I took my search to the back of the boat.

"There has to be something here," I thought *frantically searching the contents of every drawer.* I found watches, compasses, charts and directions, but no weapons. I still had the underwater lights on which gave the harbor a strange glow. I would describe it as a movie set, but I knew that this is for real. The fog had completely settled in and I was chilled to the bone. I thought that maybe there would be something in the galley, but this boat didn't have one. It's about 27 feet from end to end and about 6 feet across with just enough room to transport a few passengers if necessary.

"What are you thinking about Samantha," I scolded *myself. "Focus!"*

I tried to forget about the horror I had just witnessed AGAIN!! I tried putting the fate of my friends out of my mind for now, but what I couldn't forget was about Jonathan. Even though I loved him, I looked to the sky and cursed him for what he had done to my Mother and me. If he would have just put this boat anywhere else and stopped trying to confiscate the treasure, I wouldn't be living this hell and my friends and family would still be here with me. I was really starting to get cold now and spied one of the rain jackets hanging near the wheel, so I quickly put it on. It was the typical seaman raincoat, made of thick insulated rubber colored black and yellow. The moment I put it on, I was warmer. Of course it did not fit, it was too big, definitely sized for anyone that needs it. I started rummaging through the pockets because they were weighing me down.

"There is something in each of these ... maybe a weapon," I thought.

It wasn't a weapon, but more gold coins. There were hundreds of them, maybe more. It's not a wonder this jacket is so heavy. I knew exactly what I was going to do and moved to the rear of the boat. I leaned the upper half of my body against the railing and screamed, "Is this what you were after?" I yelled as I threw handful after handful into the harbor.

"Now leave us alone. Leave me alone, you freak! Go back to hell, where you belong!"

I'm sure that if there was anyone around, they would have thought that I was crazy. I continued shouting and emptying the pockets of the coins. I wondered how long Gregory had been collecting the treasure, because he sure had enough of them. I finished getting rid of all the coins I could find and was just standing there on the rear deck. I looked down and to the left and that's when I saw it: a diver's kit just like the one I had lost. Inside the small, blue box was a mask, a watch, and a 7 inch knife. I pulled out the knife and placed it into my jacket, and then for some reason, I fell totally apart! I had not grieved for anyone that had fallen prey to this creature, including my Father. It was probably seeing the exact same scenario that Jonathan had on our boat that triggered all these emotions. I put my elbows on the mahogany railing and buried my face into my hands. I cried and cried and I can't remember the last time that I did that. Maybe it's just because things are so very fresh in my mind, but I couldn't stop sobbing. Breathing deeply and wiping my nose on my sleeve, I couldn't believe how much pain I was in.

I had always prided myself to have the ability to take what ever life handed me, no matter what. When my parents got divorced, I didn't pass judgment or blame. I was just like... who do I see when and where? Even now I don't think any less of Jonathan because of his affair but certainly wish it hadn't happened. However, I have some regrets about a half-brother that Jonathan never shared with me. My mind flashed quickly from my Father to my friends. I remembered something special about each one of them, even Chad. It was his excitement for life that truly energized our little group. With Macy, it was her strong will, and with Jessica it was her smile and a sheer beauty she brought all of the time. My remembrances about each one of my friends caused me to start bawling again. I just couldn't believe that I would never see any of them again.

"This trip started out so great," I whispered to myself while I wiped away more tears. And I wondered what had gone wrong from my birthday party until now and really couldn't believe such a horrific scene happening over and over.

All of a sudden, I felt a whack on the back of my head and the next thing I knew, I was in the water. *"What the hell," I remember thinking.* I could taste the salt water as I floated to the surface while trying to gather my wits. I felt the force of something narrowly passing by me and then I was on the spiral sucking me towards the bottom.

"It's the devil fish," I wildly thought.

As I treaded water, I could see this strangely familiar blob rushing towards me. Thankfully, I still had on the raincoat so I reached into the pocket and pulled out the knife. It circled me again, zooming by, narrowly missing my stomach, but I felt the long legs hitting against mine. This time it did not feel like Jell-O, but more like tiny shards of glass brushing my thighs. I swam about 3 feet so that I could hold on to the ladder on the back of the boat. I wasn't afraid as much as I was pissed off.

"Come here, you weird bastard, I've got something for you," I taunted trying to get the creature to come this way. But it didn't, it came directly from the bottom and wrapped around my waist with one of its long tentacles. It could have wrapped around four or five times, but chose only twice. I still had a good grip on my knife, but was loosening my hold on the ladder. The creature was tugging ferociously trying to drag me under.

I resisted with all of my might and then had an idea. I started sawing away at the arm with the knife until it let go. There was blood in the water, but this time it was his.

"Maybe that will teach you," I shouted in that direction of the octopus.

Honestly, I didn't know where the devilfish had gone and I could not see any whirlpools in the water. I probably should have climbed aboard now, but I didn't. I decided that either I was going to kill it for it was going to kill me. It made its second attempt with more vigor than the first, by wrapping around my ankles. I wasn't ready and it successfully pulled me underwater. From what I had seen it do before, I knew its plan was to drape itself on me and feast on my skull. Rather than move away from it, I pulled it towards me. I was running out of breath and figured now was the time. I saw the gross underside of this creature. I opened my eyes, even though it burned like hell, so that I could take aim.

"You only have one shot at this Sam, don't blow it!"

I pulled the creature as close to me as I could and strangely enough, it didn't resist. Maybe it thought I had given up, but I hadn't. I was wielding the knife towards the scarlet colored creature, looking for its heart, just like Jessica told me to.

It was almost like stabbing a stretch Armstrong doll. The knife went in and I turned it 90° to the right. I really wasn't sure if I had hit the right place or not. The grip that it had on my ankles subsided and I surface for some much needed air. Holding onto the ladder, I climbed up at few steps to see my results. Having the underwater light still turned on allowed me to see the floating, lifeless devilfish floating in its own ink.

"Yeah," I yelled, "Woo Hoo!"

I felt vindicated, victorious, and exhausted. I started coughing up seawater the minute I was safely aboard. I was still wearing the jacket, but the way my adrenaline was pumping, I didn't need it. I stumbled to the radio, still clutching the knife and called the station.

Chapter 22

Epilogue

It's been at least six months, maybe more, since all this took place. My original thought about turning 30, and coming down here was almost non-existent in my mind. I've been to so many funerals, some with bodies - others without, to last me another 30 years. Yes it was shocking to meet my brother and to find out that the Father I love so much was just like a lot of other men out there. Other than loosing my friends like I did, finding out about my Father was the most disheartening event of the trip. I don't know, maybe we all think of our parents, especially the fathers, as some sort of Superman or something and when you find out that they are not, it cuts deep. Jessica, of course, had the most lavish funeral of all. There were flowers everywhere and her dad set up and endowment in her name. The endowment was to protect and discover unusual marine creatures. I don't know how they could do that after the way she died, but I guess everyone grieves in their own way. Macy and Chad had a double funeral, which I suppose is fine for their parents. If they want to think that they are together forever, who am I to disagree?

The news of the dead octopus traveled quickly around not only the island, but the globe. It was way more attention than I could have ever wanted. The media went completely overboard with this hero bullshit. If I was truly some sort of hero, my friends would still be alive. To get away from the constant glare of the cameras, I tried cutting my hair very short. It worked for a while and I got to just be myself again. I went home, not only for the funerals, but also to see my Mother. Going back to New York was dramatic enough and then you add in my new celebrity status ... it was almost overwhelming. I really don't know how true celebrities deal with this around the clock. I only did one sit-down interview on a talk show and the hostess didn't even listen to the story. She turned it from a life celebration about my three friends to some environmental crap about saving our oceans. The payment from the cruise line of almost $800,000 worth of hush money proved to not be the big story in the eyes of the media. I was so infuriated that I left.

Another surprise waiting for me back in New York City was my Mother's new boyfriend. In my opinion, this guy was too young for her. Hell, if the two of us were dating no one would look twice, but my Mother! After asking her and finding out that he was only five years older than me, my Mother and I are really got into it. She pulled the same bullshit that she used to on me and my Father. It felt good to be able to walk out of her apartment and have my sights set elsewhere. Honestly, I didn't know what I was going to do, or where I was going to go, I just knew that I was not going to stay there and had to pursue my own life. On my ride down the elevator, I had a thought and figured what the hell! The ocean was calling me. I knew people down there and could probably find a job and I certainly won't miss the winter weather.

The sun splashed beaches and cloudless sky greeted me happily, when I stepped off of the plane. *"Now, all I need is a boat and a job."*

My first move was to see Tillie. Not only to see how she was doing, since I hadn't seen her since I left and was whisked away the by authorities immediately after everything happened. I walked into that familiar, dingy police station and she wasn't there. The harbor master was there and explains to me that she had passed away.

"Oh, no, not another," I thought.

However, my spirits were raised a little when the harbor master recognized me.

"You know what you did took a lot of guts," he praised. I thanked him and was headed towards the door when out of the blue, he offered me a job. He said that he was down a man because of losing Gregory and still had not filled his vacancy. I smiled, accepted and that's how I came to be standing on my patrol boat, watching the "cruisers" frolic near the pier.

Of course the job, like any other, became routine over time, but the weather and the beautiful setting seemed to make up for it. I guess that you could say I'm really not completely settled in. I love the job, love being a local celebrity and somehow feeling a connection to my Father on this island. However, I have not purchased a home yet, so I'm still renting. Most of my time is spent patrolling the waters and watching drunks stumble along the pier on their way back to the cruise ship. Sometimes I just check out and remember Jonathan, Judy and my three friends the way we all used to be. But I suppose that everyone does that from time to time … reminisce. I find myself doing it more and more lately. It's probably part of the grieving process, don't you think? When I checked back in mentally I focused on the cruisers doing what everybody on vacation does and that's have a good time. My eyes were drawn specifically to those parasailing, I guess because it always looks like so much fun. I met a few of the guys that run the excursion and they are great people, but something else was catching my eye today. Where the people were landing was on a floating platform decorated with a bull's-eye target. The platform made ripples in the shallow water when people landed on it. It took me back to the devilfish's whirlpool that haunts me to this day. I watched ever so closely, behind my black sunglasses and I just got the feeling that something wasn't quite right. I noticed more ripples in the water about 10 yards from the platform.

"It looks like, but it can't be," I thought silently in horror. The ripples were forming a shallow whirlpool and I wondered if it was possible. My wondering abruptly came to an end with the first horrible scream."

Printed in the United States
By Bookmasters